**Maya Blake**'s hopes of becoming a writer were born when she picked up her first romance at thirteen. Little did she know her dream would come true! Does she still pinch herself every now and then to make sure it's not a dream? Yes, she does! Feel free to pinch her, too, via Twitter, Facebook or Goodreads! Happy reading!

# BOUND BY MY SCANDALOUS PREGNANCY

MAYA BLAKE

**MILLS & BOON**

# CHAPTER ONE

REINCARNATION. KARMA. SINS coming home to roost.

Once upon a time, in the not-too-distant past, if anyone had asked me if I believed in any of those things I'd have rolled my eyes and told them to get real. That life worked on the amount of effort you put into each day.

On love.

Loyalty.

Hard work.

How wrong I was.

Frozen outside the towering glass and steel offices of one of the most powerful men on the globe, my wrists tingling from the phantom handcuffs that might become real before the hour was out, I wondered which deity I'd wronged to bring me to this end.

Did it even matter that the domino effect of sheer rotten luck mostly had nothing to do with me? Was it worth ranting that the sins of the father shouldn't be visited upon the daughter?

No.

The awful truth was, while the majority of what happened to me in the past few years wasn't my fault, this last, shocking misstep was one hundred percent mine.

Sure, I could prove that a collection of things had culminated in that one gigantic error, but the reality was inescapable. The buck, and the blame, stopped with me.

*Time to own it, Sadie.*

*One more minute*, I silently pleaded to whatever higher power held my fate in its cruel grip.

But, adding to every other misfortune unfolding in my life, my plea went unheeded.

The two sharply dressed security guards who'd been

eyeing me with increasing wariness through the imposing glass frontage were heading my way. These days the whole world was on edge. I of all people should know that.

The economy had been partly responsible for decimating the family I once took for granted. The family currently hanging by a very fragile thread.

And dressed in threadbare clothes that were at least five seasons old, my troubled expression reflected in the polished glass, I wouldn't be surprised if I was wrestled to the ground and arrested for trespassing. Or worse.

Disturbingly, that possibility gleamed palatably for a second, attesting to my true state of mind. *Really?* I'd rather be arrested than—

'Excuse me, miss. Can I help you?'

I jumped, my hand flying to my throat to contain the heart beating itself into a frenzy. The burlier of the two guards had stepped through the revolving doors without my noticing and now stood a few feet away. Everything about him promised he could switch from courteous to menacing in a heartbeat.

*Definitely time to own it, Sadie.*

'I…' I stopped, moved my tongue to wet desert-dry lips. 'I need to see Mr Xenakis. Is he in?'

His eyes narrowed. 'You'll have to ask for him at the reception desk. Do you have an appointment?'

I nearly laughed. How could I make an appointment to confess what I'd done?

'Um, no. But—'

'I think you should leave now, miss.' His tone indicated it wasn't a suggestion.

'Please! It's a matter of life or death.'

He froze. 'Whose life?'

I bit the inside of my lip, afraid I'd overexaggerated things a little. For all I knew, the man I'd wronged wouldn't bat an eyelid at my actions. Truth was, I wouldn't know until I confronted him.

'I… I can't tell you. But it's urgent. And private. If you could just tell me if Mr Xenakis is in?'

For an interminable minute he simply watched me. Then he grasped my elbow. 'Come with me, Miss…?'

I hesitated. Once I gave my name there'd be no going back. But what choice did I have? Either confess and plead my case or wait for the authorities to show up at my door. 'Preston. Sadie Preston.'

With swift efficiency, I was ushered across the stunning atrium of Xenakis Aeronautics, through a series of nondescript doors that led to the bowels of the basement and into a room bearing all the hallmarks of an interrogation chamber.

Hysteria threatened. I suppressed it as the guard muttered a stern, 'Stay here.'

The next twenty minutes were the longest of my life. In direct contrast to the speed with which my life flashed before my eyes after the enormity of what I'd done sank in.

The man who entered the room then was even more imposing, leaving me in no doubt that my request was being taken seriously. And not in a good way.

'Miss Preston?'

At my hesitant nod, the tall, salt-and-pepper-haired man held the door open, his dark eyes assessing me even more thoroughly once I scrambled to my feet.

'I'm Wendell, head of Mr Xenakis's security team. This way,' he said, in a voice that brooked no argument.

Dear God, either Neo Xenakis was super thorough about his interactions with the common man or he was paranoid about his security. Neither boded well.

Another series of incongruous underground hallways brought us to a steel-framed lift. Wendell accessed it with a sleek black key card. Once inside, he pressed another button.

The lift shot up, leaving my stomach and the last dregs of my courage on the basement floor. I wanted to throw myself at the lift doors, claw them open and jump out, consequences be damned. But my feet were paralysed with the unshakeable acceptance that I would only be postponing the inevitable.

Besides, I didn't run from my responsibilities. Not like my father literally had when things got tough. Not like my mother was doing by burying her head in the sand and frivolously gambling away money we didn't have. A habit that had veered scarily towards addiction in the last six months.

I stifled my anxiety as the lift slid to a smooth halt.

One problematic mountain at a time.

This particular one bore all the hallmarks of an Everest climb. One that might only see me to Base Camp before the worst happened.

Not a single member of the sharply dressed staff I'd spotted coming and going downstairs roamed this rarefied space, which boasted the kind of furnishings that graced the expensive designer magazines my mother had avidly subscribed to back when money had been no object for the Prestons. The kind that had always made me wonder if the pictures were staged or if people actually lived like that.

Evidently, they did.

The dove-grey carpeting looked exclusive and expensive, making me cringe as my scuffed, cheap shoes trod over it. Lighter shades of grey silk graced the walls, with stylish lampshades illuminating the space and the twin console tables that stood on either side of the immense double doors.

Made of white polished ash, with handles that looked like gleaming aeroplane wings, everything about them and the glimpse of the expansive conference rooms I could see from where I stood screamed opulence and exclusivity. The type that belonged to owners who didn't take kindly to strangers ruining their day with the sort of news I had to deliver.

Sweat broke out on my palms. Before I could perform the undignified act of rubbing them against the polyester weave of my skirt, Wendell knocked twice.

The voice that beckoned was deep enough to penetrate the solid wood, formidable enough to raise the dread digging its claws into me…and enigmatic enough to send a skitter of…*something else* down my spine.

That unknown quality threatened to swamp all other emotions as Wendell opened the doors. 'You have five minutes,' he informed me, then stepped to one side.

The need to flee resurged. How long would a prison sentence be for this kind of crime, anyway?

Too long. My mother wouldn't survive more upheaval. And with our landlord threatening eviction, the last thing I could afford was more turbulence.

With no choice but to face my fate, I took a shaky step into the office.

And promptly lost every last gasp of air from my lungs at the sight of the man braced against the floor-to-ceiling glass windows, arms crossed and fierce eyes locked on me.

If his surroundings screamed ultraexclusivity and supreme wealth, the man himself was so many leagues above that station, he required his own stratosphere. Even stationary, he vibrated with formidable power—the kind that commanded legions with just one look.

And his body…

The navy suit, clearly bespoke, enhanced the bristling power of his athletic build. Like his impressive six-foot-plus height, his wide tapered shoulders seemed to go on for ever, with the kind of biceps that promised to carry any load rippling beneath the layers of clothes. Above the collar of his pristine white shirt, his square jaw jutted out with unapologetic masculinity, and his pure alpha-ness was not in any way diluted by the dimple in his chin. If anything, that curiously arresting feature only drew deeper attention to the rest of his face. To the haughty cheekbones resting beneath narrowed eyes, his wide forehead and the sensual slash of his lips.

He was…indescribable. Because words like *attractive* or *breathtaking* or even *magnificent* didn't do him nearly enough justice.

And as he continued to appraise me, every last ounce of my courage threatened to evaporate as surely as my breath. Because the way he stared at me, as if he found me as fascinating as I found him, sent a spiralling wave of pure, unadulterated awareness charging through me.

For some inexplicable reason my hair seemed to hold singular appeal for him, making me almost feel as if he was touching the tied back tresses, caressing the strands between his fingers.

The snick of the door shutting made me flinch—a reaction he spotted immediately as his arms dropped and he began to prowl slowly towards me.

Sweet heaven, even the way he moved was spectacular. I'd never truly comprehended the term 'poetry in motion.' Until now.

*Focus, Sadie. You're not here to ogle the first billionaire you've ever met.*

I opened my mouth to speak. He beat me to it.

'Whoever you are, you seem to have caught Wendell in a good mood. I don't believe he's allowed anyone to walk in off the street and demand to see me in…well, *ever*,' he rasped in a gravel-rolling-in-honey voice, sending another cascade of pure sensation rushing over my skin.

Momentarily thrown by the effect of his voice, I couldn't tell if his tone suggested he'd be having a word with Wendell later about that misstep or if the whole thing simply amused him. He was that enigmatic to read. The mystery stretched my already oversensitive nerves, triggering my babble-when-nervous flaw.

'That was Wendell in a *good* mood? I shudder to think what he's like in a bad mood,' I blurted. Then I cringed harder when the meaning of my words sank in.

*Oh, no…*

His eyes narrowed even further as he stopped several feet away from me. 'Perhaps you'd like to move whatever this is along?'

Impatience coated his tone even as his eyes raked a closer inspection over my body, pausing on the frayed thinness of my blouse, the slightly baggy cut of my skirt following my recent weight loss, before dropping to my legs. The return journey was just as sizzling. Hell, more so.

That stain of inadequacy, of not being worthy—which had dogged me from the moment my father's abscondment-announcing postcard had landed on the front doormat, in shocking synchronicity with the bailiff's arrival on our doorstep eight years ago—flared like a fever.

I didn't need one of my mother's magazines to tell me that this man didn't meddle with the likes of me...*ever*.

It was in every delicious frame of his impeccable body, every measured exhalation and every flicker of those sooty, spiky eyelashes that most women would pay hundreds to replicate. He would date socialites with faultless pedigree. Heiresses with flawless bone structure who listed royalty as close friends.

Not the callously abandoned daughter of a disgraced middle-grade financier and an almost-addicted gambler, whose only nod to the arts was learning how to execute a half-decent jeté in year-five ballet.

'Or do you feel inclined to use your five minutes in melo-dramatic silence?' he drawled.

The realisation that I'd been gaping at him brought a spike of embarrassment. 'I'm not being melodramatic.'

One brow hiked, and his gaze scanned me from top to toe again before his face slowly hardened.

'You stated that you needed to see me as a matter of life or death, but between the time you set foot in my building and your arrival in my office I've ascertained that every member of my family is safe and accounted for. My em-ployees' well-being will take longer, and a lot of manpower to establish, so if I'm being pranked I'd caution you to turn around and leave right now—'

'This isn't about your present family. It's about your future one.'

He turned to stone. A quite miraculous thing since he was such a big, towering force of a man whose aura threw off electric charges. His ability not to move a muscle would have been fascinating to watch if I hadn't been terrified of the look in his eyes. The one that promised chaos and doom.

'Repeat that, if you please.'

I couldn't. Not if I valued my life.

'I… Perhaps I need to start from the beginning.'

A single clench to his jaw. 'Start *somewhere*. And fast. I'm not a patient man, Miss Preston. And I'm about to be late for an important meeting.'

My rib-banging heart rate shuddered in terror.

My life flashed before my eyes. *Again.*

I pushed away disturbingly bleak images of a life unfulfilled and dreams dashed. Curled my sweaty fists tighter and cleared my throat.

'My name is Sadie Preston…' When that only prompted a higher arch of his brow I hurried on. 'I work…*worked* at the Phoenix Clinic.'

Right until I was summarily fired, three hours ago. But the problem of my unemployment would have to be addressed later. Provided I didn't end up in jail—

My train of thought screeched to a halt as he rocked forward, slid his hands into his trouser pockets and brought muscular thighs into singeing relief. Time pulsed by in silence as the very masculine stance ramped up the heat running through me.

'For your sake, I hope this isn't some sort of misguided attempt to garner employment, because I can assure you—'

'It's not!' My interruption was much more shrill than I'd intended. And I knew immediately that neither it nor my tone had gained me any favours. Hell, his imposing presence seemed to loom even larger in the vast office, his aura terrifying. 'Please…if you would just hear me out?'

'*You're* the one who seems to be tongue-tied, Miss Preston. While *my* precious time bleeds away. So let me make this easy for you. You have one minute to state your business. I advise you to make it worthwhile, for both our sakes.'

*Or what?*

For a single moment I feared I'd blurted the words, the volatile mix of annoyance and trepidation having finally broken me. But he didn't seem any more incandescent. Simply terribly hacked off at my continued delay in spilling the beans.

'I was fired this morning because…' *pause, deep breath* '…because I accidentally destroyed your…' I squeezed my eyes shut. When I opened them, he was still there, breathtaking and immovable as a marble statue.

Firm, sensually curved lips flattened. 'My what?' he demanded tersely.

Tension vibrated through me as I forced my vocal cords to work. 'I destroyed…your…your stored sperm sample.'

For a horribly tense minute he simply stared at me with utter confusion—as if he couldn't quite comprehend my words—and then that face that defied description tautened into a mask of pure, cold disbelief.

'You. Did. What?'

It wasn't shouted. Or whispered. It was even toned. And absolutely deadly.

I shivered from head to toe, severely doubting my ability ever to speak again as I opened my mouth and words failed to emerge.

Terrifying seconds ticked away as we stood in rigid silence, gazes locked.

'Speak,' he commanded, again without so much as any inflexion in his voice. His lips had gone white with grim fury and he was barely breathing.

I prised my tongue from the roof of my mouth. To do what I'd come here to do. Appeal to his better nature.

Taking a hesitant step towards him, I tried a small smile. 'Mr Xenakis—'

One hand erupted from his pocket in a halting motion. 'Do not attempt to cajole. Do not attempt to prevaricate. I want the facts. Bare and immediate.'

This time his voice had altered. It was a primordial rumble. Like the nape-tingling premonition before a cataclysmic event.

My smile evaporated. 'When I arrived at work this morning…' *late because of my mother and another futile attempt to get through to her* '… I was given a list of samples to dispose of. I… It's not part of my job description, but—'

'What is your *actual* job at the Phoenix Clinic?' The barest hint of an accent had thickened his voice, making him impossibly sexier.

'I'm a receptionist.'

It was the only half-decent paying job I could find that would support my mother and me until I figured out a way to help her out of her dark tunnel of despair and resume the marketing degree I'd suspended so I could care for her.

'And what business does a receptionist have handling patient samples?'

His tone was a chilling blade of reason. He wasn't furious. Not yet, anyway. Right now Neo Xenakis was on a cold, fact-finding mission.

I managed to answer. 'It's not the usual procedure, but we were severely short-staffed today and the list I was given stated that the samples had already been triple-checked.'

'Obviously not. Or you wouldn't be here, would you?' he rasped.

A wave of shame hit me. My error could have been avoided if I hadn't been so frazzled. If I hadn't been worried that my mother and I were about to lose the roof over our heads. If my boss's medical secretary hadn't called in sick, leaving *me* as temporary—and infinitely unlucky—cover.

About to attempt another pleading of my case, I froze when a loud buzz sounded from his desk.

For the longest time he stared at me, as if trying to decipher whether or not everything I'd told him was some sort of hoax.

When the intercom sounded again, he strode to his desk with unbridled impatience. 'Yes?' he grated.

'There's a Spencer Donnelly on the line for you, sir. He says it's urgent.'

My breath caught. He heard it and speared me with narrow-eyed speculation. To his assistant, he said, 'I don't believe I know a Spencer Donnelly. Who is he?'

I stepped forward, earning myself more intense scrutiny. 'That's my boss. My ex-boss, I mean. I think he's calling you to explain.'

And most likely to ensure the blame stayed squarely on my shoulders.

Neo hit the mute button. 'Is he responsible for what happened?' he demanded from me.

'Not…not directly. But he's the head of the clinic—'

'I don't care what his role is. I care about who's directly responsible. Are you saying it was you and you alone?'

My nape heated at the imminent fall of the axe, but seeing as there was nothing more I could do but admit my total culpability, I nodded. 'Yes. It was my fault.'

His nostrils flared as he unmuted the line. 'Take a message,' he informed his assistant, then sauntered back to where I stood.

For another stomach-churning minute he pinned me beneath his gaze. 'Tell me what your intention was in coming here, Miss Preston,' he invited silkily.

His even voice did not soothe me for one second. Whatever his reason for depositing a sperm sample at a fertility clinic, the consequences of my mistake would be brutal.

Alternate heat and cold flashed through my veins. I would have given everything I owned to be able to flee from his presence. But, seeing as fate and circumstance had already taken everything from me, leaving me with very little of value…

'I thought you deserved to hear the truth from me. And also my a-apology,' I said, my throat threatening to close up at the look on his face.

He said nothing, simply waited for several seconds before he elevated that characterful eyebrow, his silent sarcasm announcing that I hadn't actually proffered any apology.

I cursed the heat rushing gleefully into my face at his icy mockery as he saw what he was doing to me. 'I… I'm sorry, Mr Xenakis. I didn't mean to destroy your property. If there was a way to undo it, I would…' I stopped, knowing the words were useless. There was no reversing what I'd done.

'And I'm simply to let you off the hook, am I? Based on you doing the honourable thing by coming here to throw yourself on my mercy?'

What could I say to that? 'I know it's a lot to ask, but I promise I didn't mean to.'

His gaze dropped and I caught the faintest shake of his head as a wave of disbelief flared over his face again. For the longest time he stared at the carpet, his jaw clenching and unclenching as he fought whatever emotion gripped him so tightly.

In that moment, my senses wanted to do the unthinkable and put myself in his shoes—but, no. I couldn't afford to get emotionally carried away.

If, by some cruel twist of fate, there was something wrong with Neo Xenakis's reproductive equipment, wouldn't he have seemed a little…*desolate*, somehow, instead of looking as if he could go toe to toe with Zeus? And win?

Several expressions flitted across his features, too fast to decipher. But when he lifted his gaze to mine once more, chilling premonition swept over me.

Mr Donnelly had known I wouldn't be let off scot-free, which was why he'd insisted I be the first in the line of fire in admitting culpability. The hurried internet search I'd done on the bus ride into the city had left me reeling at the enormity of the adversary I'd unwittingly created with one fatalistic click of the mouse.

Neo Xenakis regarded me with the flat coldness of a cobra about to strike. 'You *didn't mean to*? That applies when you tread on someone's foot. Or accidentally spill your coffee at an inopportune moment. Correct me if I'm wrong, but the Phoenix Clinic has a stringent set of checks in place, does it not?'

I opened my mouth to answer, but he was shaking his head, already rejecting my confirmation.

'Whatever you thought was going to happen with your coming here, I'm afraid it won't be that easy, Miss Preston.'

'What do you mean?'

God, did he want me to beg? Fall on my face and prostrate myself before him?

The weirdest thought entered my head. That however he intended me to pay, it would be welcome. Perhaps even a little...*life-changing.*

When his gaze dropped to my parted lips I entertained the notion, while staring at his mouth, that whatever those reparations were they would be *carnal* in nature. That I would perhaps even...*enjoy it.*

*Sweet heaven, Sadie. What's wrong with you?*

Dragging my focus from the lush curve of his lips, I met his gaze—only to find the grey depths alight with the same blaze that singed my blood.

Abruptly he turned away, returned to his desk and picked up a sleek-looking tablet. 'Willa, please come in.'

Confusion mingled with those peculiar feelings rioted through me, rendering me speechless as the door opened and a stylishly dressed blonde entered. The woman was more suited to traipse down a runway than give executive assistance. The dismissive glance she threw me before sashaying her way to her boss's desk said she was well aware of her assets.

'Yes, Mr Xenakis.' Unsurprisingly, her voice dripped with sensual interest as she smiled at him.

Curbing my instant dislike for Willa, I listened to them exchange a low-voiced conversation about his upcoming meeting before he rounded his desk.

'Escort Miss Preston to my penthouse. She's to stay there until I'm done with my meeting. If she attempts to leave, inform Wendell.'

My irritation at being discussed as if I wasn't there doubled at the edict he'd just delivered. 'What? You can't... I won't just stay here at your whim!'

The fury he'd kept at bay finally flared into singeing life. 'You've destroyed my property, Miss Preston, making your actions a crime. Attempt to leave and I'll be forced to let the authorities handle it. You have two options. Stay and discuss this further, after my meeting. Or leave and face the consequences.' He strode towards the door, throwing over his shoulder, 'I'll let you inform Willa of your decision.'

Then he was gone.

I veered towards the windows, hoping for a ray of enlightenment. But the typical English weather had greyed in complete alignment with my circumstances.

I couldn't leave. Not unless I wanted to risk worsening my situation.

Neo Xenakis was in shock, still grappling with the news. Would he show mercy when he'd calmed down? Was I better off handing myself over to the authorities and pleading my case with a lawyer through the courts?

With what funds? Even before I lost my job we were barely scraping by. I didn't have the resources to pay a lawyer for even ten minutes of his time!

I was better off waiting. Perhaps talking him round to getting him to return to the clinic to deposit another sample...

Willa's pointed throat-clearing triggered a wince. Turning, I lifted my chin and met her contemptuous stare.

'I'll stay,' I announced, with as much firmness as I could manage, considering my stomach had gone into a thousand-foot free fall.

# CHAPTER TWO

*RETREAT. REGROUP.*

For the dozenth time in what felt like the longest afternoon of my life, I shook my head.

'You don't agree, Mr Xenakis?'

I refocused on the leader of the Brazilian marketing team gathered around the conference table and wondered what I'd missed while my brain was stuck in that endless cycle of life-altering words uttered by the most captivating creature I'd ever seen.

*I'm sorry... I've destroyed...everything.*

To think I'd been convinced she was pranking me. Or, even more amusing, that she had latched on to an inventive method of getting my attention, since most feminine ploys left me cold these days.

My steep drop in interest in the opposite sex hadn't gone unnoticed in recent years. Socialites who'd smugly decided they were an integral part of my healing process were scratching their heads, wondering why I'd permanently lost their numbers. Heiresses who'd eagerly and blatantly sought an alliance with the newly *un*engaged Xenakis bachelor were left stunned as every avenue of contact was firmly rebuffed.

It hadn't even been worth the time to inform them that the thrill of the chase had stopped being, well...*thrilling.* That the eighteen months I'd spent sowing every wild oat I could had left me ashen mouthed and even more jaded than I'd been when I woke up in that hospital to the cruellest betrayal.

To think I'd imagined *that* was the worst moment of my life.

The stark reality of Sadie Preston's presence in my penthouse—as per Willa's confirmation, minutes ago—attested to that moment having well and truly been usurped.

Was this how my brother Axios had felt when presented with the noose-like proposition he'd faced almost a year ago?

No, Ax's sentence was finite. It would end…or rather should have been ending in a matter of weeks, had his bride of fewer than twenty-four hours not fled from him and vanished without a trace, leaving him bewildered and stuck in limbo.

*Christos. If he's feeling even a fraction of what I'm feeling now…*

But then the bride he'd acquired hadn't been wanted. Whereas what Sadie Preston had taken from me was… *priceless.*

The dreaded cancer diagnosis which had precipitated my sperm donation in anticipation of radiation might have turned out to be a false alarm when I was twenty-five, but the scars marring my skin beneath my clothes were a reminder of why that visit to the Phoenix Clinic had turned out to be a pivotal, life-affirming event for me. A light in the bleak darkness of the blissful ignorance I'd lived in for almost a year, before the blindfold had been ripped from my eyes almost as ruthlessly as the accident that had attempted to rob me of my life.

Anger and pure, unadulterated disbelief flashed like lightning through my system. I shook my head again, aware that I was attracting bewildered stares from the marketing gurus I'd hired to promote the interests of Xenakis Aeronautics in Brazil.

It had taken a draining amount of mental dexterity to get through my other two meetings, and now a quick glance at the presentation slide brought me up to speed with what I'd missed. Or rather, what *they'd* missed.

'This isn't going to work. Besides being unexceptional, you've aimed it at the wrong demographic.'

The team leader nodded enthusiastically. 'Which demographic were you thinking of, Mr Xenakis?'

I stopped myself from rolling my eyes. Was I required to do *all* their work for them? 'You have the data from the beta test. From what I'm seeing, you haven't bothered to consult it. I'm not seeing any application of the feedback we received from millennials with children.'

My chest clenched as another percussive wave of shock pummelled me. Children. Families. *Fatherhood.*

A state I'd never experience now, thanks to the actions of a redhead whose lips had dripped words of remorse but whose attitude vaunted defiance. Those startling green eyes had dared me to *bring it on* even as her bedroom voice wobbled with apology.

That little chin had been raised in silent combat, displaying the silken skin of her throat and a shadow of cleavage. And as for the other treasures hidden beneath her cheap, threadbare clothes…and that hair I wanted to wrap my fist around…

Theos mou. *Get a grip.*

It was searing shock that had stopped me from instructing Wendell to hand her over to the authorities as soon as she'd confessed her crime.

And shock was the reason she was in my penthouse while I bought myself some time to deal with the earth-shattering news. Besides, as much as I trusted my security chief, some things were private. And this matter couldn't get more private.

Sadie Preston had essentially taken every last shred of hope for my future and trashed it. And the worst thing was that I hadn't known how much the nebulous prospect of fatherhood had meant until any chance of it had been destroyed—first with betrayal and lies, and then with a careless press of the delete button on a computer.

My chest growing tighter, I jerked to my feet, the need to do something clawing through me. 'Ladies and gentlemen, I trust we know which direction we're heading for in the campaign now?' At their nods of assent, I headed for the door. 'You have one week to get it right. Don't let me down.'

*Don't let me down.*

Was I wasting my breath, saying that? Was I doomed to be disappointed in everyone I put my trust in? Be it in personal stakes or in a supposedly exclusive, top-of-the-range clinic?

My mouth soured as I strode for the lift.

The Brazilian contingent only needed a little guidance—they'd come through eventually. If they didn't, they'd simply be…replaced.

While I… Christos, *I would never be a father.*

I braced a hand against the wall, the weight of reality attempting to crush my shoulders.

So what if in the past I'd had my doubts about my potential effectiveness as a father? Xenakis men were many things, but exemplary fathers they were not. My grandfather had buried himself in work up to the point when he'd dropped dead of a heart attack, trying to save his near-bankrupt family. And long before that, my father had been denied his father's favour, resulting in the neglect of his own family.

While we tolerated each other now, for the sake of the family business, I didn't have a single memory of any bonding experience with my father. Boarding school had taken care of my formative years, followed by a gruelling apprenticeship at Xenakis Aeronautics.

I had respect and loyalty, earned from my position.

But affection? Or, hell, *love*?

In light of the bombshell that had flattened my life three hours ago, even the fake-it-till-you-make-it plan I'd so loftily believed would work with any future offspring had been shattered.

The finger I lifted to press the lift button shook with the force of the loss raking my insides. The moment I was inside the cubicle I attempted to breathe through the anguish, to get myself back under control.

Not even when Anneka had shown her true colours that day in the hospital three years ago had such a sense of deep loss affected me. While her betrayal had been similarly life altering, deep down a part of me had been thankful to have been given the opportunity to cut her out of my life before she truly sank her claws into me. Sure, my male pride had smarted for well over a year after she'd made a fool of me—cue excessive wild oat sowing—but ultimately, I'd escaped her trap.

With this there was not a single upside.

Save perhaps making the culprit pay?

The notion had gathered considerable pace by the time I entered my penthouse.

She stood at the glass window, her attention on the view. At some point between leaving the conference room only minutes ago and now, the sun had decided to shine. It threw a halo over her, turning her hair into living flames. Tendrils had slipped their loose knots, and as I watched she absently tucked a strand over her ear, slid her hand over her nape, then her shoulder, to massage it in firm, circular strokes.

The action sent another wave of tension through me, drawing my attention to her translucent skin, to the perfection of her hourglass figure and the stunning legs framed against the glass. Her other hand was splayed against it as if she yearned for the freedom beyond. Sensing my presence, she whirled around, those endless pools of green going wide at the sight of me.

'Oh… I had no idea you'd returned.'

My lips tightened, and that percussive mix of anger and desolation threatened again. 'I believe it's your lack of awareness that has led us to this point.'

She had the audacity to look hurt. The surrealness of it nearly made me shake my head again—but *enough*. I was done with being confounded. The important thing was how to proceed from here.

Doctors. Specialists. Investigate one final time.

Every option left a trail of displeasure, and the prospect of having my dire circumstances prodded was even more unwelcome than the verdict I'd woken to after a three-week coma three years ago: the severity of my skiing accident meant that I couldn't father children naturally. That my only hope of becoming a father rested on a sperm sample donated years ago, when I'd faced another crisis.

*A seemingly miraculous turn of events that was now crushed to nothing.*

Sadie Preston fidgeted where she stood, even as that pert little nose started to rise.

*Christos*, had no one ever taught this creature the concept of true contrition? But she wasn't as calm as she attempted to look. Her chest rose and fell in gathering agitation, and her small feet were curling and uncurling within the cheap flat shoes she wore. The action highlighted the smooth definition of her calves, and against my will I dropped my gaze, the better to absorb it.

When that only prompted a sharp need to test their suppleness beneath my fingers, I turned, made a beeline for my drinks cabinet. A dash of Hine in the crystal tumbler clutched in my hand brought a little clarity.

At the delicate throat-clearing behind me, I squeezed my eyes shut for a control-gathering second. Before I turned, she was speaking.

'I know you only need to look at me to remember why I'm here. What I've done. But I've been thinking… If you wouldn't mind giving me a little information, maybe we can put our heads together and come up with a solution.'

Another urge to laugh this away in the hope that it was some extended acid dream hit me. '"*Put our heads together*"? Why would we want to do that? Are you a doctor?'

Rose-red lips compressed, drawing my attention to yet another tempting part of her body.

*The body of your nemesis.*

'You know I'm not. I'm just trying to help—'

'I think you've done quite enough, don't you? Imagine we are the last two people on earth. Then be assured that I would rather take my chances with whatever apocalypse I face than accept *your* help.'

Her translucent skin lost a shade of colour. 'Do you need to be so cruel?' she muttered.

Absurdly, that plaintive question sent an arrow of guilt through me. *Theos mou.* What the hell was going on? Was it Upside Down Day? I downed half my drink, hoping the alcohol would burn through the fog.

The hope was in vain. So I approached until we stood half a dozen feet apart. 'Fine. Humour me. How would you propose we "put our heads together"?'

'Well, I was thinking that if you wouldn't mind telling me the circumstances behind your needing to use the Phoenix Clinic the first time around—'

'No, I would not. Next scenario.'

She hesitated, the tip of her pink tongue darting out to wet her lower lip. This time the punch in my gut was purely carnal. Ravenous. Demanding. *Lustful.*

For *this* woman? *Christos*, the world had truly turned upside down!

'Okay. If you're in a position to deposit another sample, perhaps I could contribute financially towards the future storage?'

Bitterness and bleakness lanced me in equal spikes. 'You don't look as if you can afford decent attire, let alone the fees of a clinic that charges upward of six figures. Do you have secret access to a gold mine, Sadie Preston? Or clairvoyant insight to the next set of lottery numbers?'

Her eyes flashed. 'Has anyone ever told you it's a mistake to judge a book by its cover?'

'If I am misjudging you, I'll consider rendering you an apology. Am I?'

She managed to hold my gaze for all of three seconds before her eyes dropped. Against her smooth cheeks, her long, unadorned eyelashes fanned in a seductive curl, highlighting her delicate eyelids. The combination of delicate, defiant and alluring made me grip my glass harder. But, more than that, I wanted her to lift her gaze, to show me those hypnotic green pools once again.

When she did, my breath caught.

*I was attracted to her.*

This woman, who'd brought me news of an apocalyptic kind, had awakened a libido grown so jaded I'd set it on the back burner in favour of pursuing even more success in the challenging boardrooms of Xenakis Aeronautics.

Was it the heightened bleakness of it all triggering this? And why was I wasting time deciphering it when I had no intention of following through on it?

'No, you're not wrong. I can't afford to foot the bill now. But perhaps we can come to an agreement?'

*Here it comes. The age-old proposition.*

The idea that she would offer herself to me on a platter drew deep disappointment. Enough to make me down the rest of my drink in abject resignation.

'Enlighten me about this agreement.'

'I'm two semesters away from completing a marketing degree. I've been top of my class every year. I can maybe work for your company from when I'm done? Pay you back that way?'

Surprise jolted me, followed by the familiar echo of wanting something because I'd been denied it. Had I *wanted* her on a platter? More specifically in my bed?

*Yes!*

I ignored the blaring affirmation, concentrated on what she'd said. So she wasn't just a simple receptionist.

The determination stamped across her face almost made

me believe her. *Almost.* For all I knew she was just spinning tales. Just as Anneka had spun lies around our relationship until an unguarded phone conversation had revealed the depths of her deplorable nature and the lengths she'd been prepared to go to ensure she received an unrivalled payday.

'How old are you?'

The mutinous look that crossed her face said she was debating not answering. Perhaps suggesting I mind my own business. But she realised very quickly that the question pertained to the proposal she was making.

'I'm twenty-five,' she offered, with clear reluctance.

'Most twenty-five-year-olds are done with their education.'

'My circumstances are different. I had to interrupt my education for personal reasons.'

Reasons she clearly wasn't about to disclose. I hid my disgruntlement. For now. 'Why a receptionist? Why not a paid internship in your chosen field?'

Impatience crossed her face. 'With respect, my reasons are private. But what I've said can easily be verified with my university professors.'

*Enough.* This had gone on long enough. 'You walked in off the street to confess a crime. As admirable as you seem to think admitting your culpability should be, I have zero reason to trust you. Not with my personal property and certainly not with my business. Your offer is declined.'

She inhaled sharply, the action drawing my attention to her chest. To her parted lips. *Christos.*

'So that's it? You're going to throw me to the wolves?'

'For what you've done? Yes, Sadie Preston. That's exactly what I'm going to do.'

Despite his doom-filled decree, he didn't move.

In the hours I'd been stuck in his opulent penthouse, one question had persistently swarmed my mind—why did a man whose every breath and expression spelled out his masculine potency and unapologetic virility need to store a sperm sample?

Eventually, curiosity had got the better of me. And the internet had been breathlessly efficient in providing high-resolution digital answers.

'Is this to be a staring contest?' he mused now, in a bone-dry tone tinged with that note I'd mistaken for bleakness earlier when I delivered my news. 'You're attempting to hypnotise me into reversing my verdict, perhaps?'

'What if I am?' I parried. If he was about to throw me to the wolves, what did I have to lose?

One corner of his mouth twitched with stark amusement. But then his face settled into a hard mask. My heart lurched. With every breath I wished I could go back, take my time, pay better attention—even with Mr Donnelly's unpleasant presence hovering over me.

But it was too late.

The damage had been done.

Neo Xenakis took another step closer, bringing that hard-packed body brimming with tensile, barely leashed power into my space. I wanted to step back, flatten myself against the glass wall, but that would exhibit a weakness I couldn't afford to show.

The internet had supplied ample examples of his shark-like business savvy too. This was a man who relished challenge. He'd never step into the arena with a weaker opponent, and the inevitable victory of his trouncing bigger targets was all the sweeter for it.

Was that why I didn't look away?

Was that why I even dared to clench my jaw and all but urge him to do his worst?

Because I wanted him to conquer me?

White-hot sensation flashed through me, made my nape tingle and my body blaze with the same anticipation I'd felt earlier, even before I knew that he'd entered the room. That misplaced illicit thrill that had ratcheted higher when

I turned around to find him watching me with those hooded eyes containing an indecipherable gleam.

Here it was again, eating me alive when all I needed to do was hold my tongue and continue to demonstrate appropriate contrition.

For how long, though? And then what?

He'd given his verdict. Clemency was off the table. And yet, despite what he'd said about throwing me to the wolves, he seemed in the mood to play with me. Seemed perfectly content to indulge in the staring contest he'd ridiculed moments ago.

'Would it work?' I asked.

*Dear God. Be quiet, Sadie. Just shut—*

To my eternal shame, my stomach chose that pithy moment to announce its intense hunger.

Neo Xenakis's gaze dropped to my belly at the unladylike growl, then returned to mine with a dark frown. 'When was the last time you ate?'

I shrugged. 'I don't remember. It doesn't matter.'

'It matters if I wish to enjoy my evening drink without your digestive system providing accompanying acoustics.'

Heat burned my face. 'I… I had a coffee this morning.'

His frown deepened. 'That's all you've had all day? It's six in the evening.'

'I know what time it is, Mr Xenakis.'

He raised a brow at my crisp tone. I wasn't about to admit I'd gone into the office with hopes of snagging a stray Danish left over from the early-morning client meeting, only to be confronted by an incandescent Mr Donnelly before I could satisfy my raging hunger. After that, fear and panic had eroded my appetite. Until now, evidently.

Neo Xenakis regarded me with quiet intensity, weighing his decision for a terse moment. Then his lips flattened. 'Far be it from me to send a criminal to the gallows on an empty stomach. Shall I instruct my chef to set another place for dinner, or are you in a hurry to face your crimes?' he drawled.

*Bite your tongue, Sadie!*

'That depends. Do you intend to torture me for the rest of the evening by recounting just how your wolves are going to tear me apart?'

'You think you know what torture is?' he asked, with a veil of deadly calm that didn't fool me for a second.

I'd inconvenienced him, angered him by necessitating a return trip to the clinic to make a second deposit, when he'd much rather be occupied with other things. Like dating another supermodel.

And he wasn't in a mood to let it go.

'There are only so many times I can say I'm sorry. It's clear you're not going to forgive me or tell me what I can do to make this right. Right now I'm failing to see how joining you for dinner improves my circumstances.'

'It could simply be an act of further character exploration on my part. To tell me which way I should lean in the punishment scales. Unlike you, I don't wish to undertake that task on an empty stomach. But, of course, your options are very much yours to take.'

Oh, how cunning of him. That insidious need to surrender to his will swept over me. I resisted by squaring my shoulders. 'Then I guess that's fine. If that's the only way to progress this…discussion.'

The merest hint of a smile twitched his lips. Then, seeming almost stunned by the action, he scowled.

Not the most enthusiastic response I'd ever had to meal-sharing, but I imagined under the circumstances a beggar couldn't be a chooser.

For another short second he stared at me, as if debating the wisdom of his offer. Then abruptly he crossed the vast, magnificently decorated living room to a dainty-legged console table, picked up a phone and relayed a message in rapid-fire Greek.

Finished, he set his glass down. 'Come.'

The command was quiet, but powerful enough to propel me forward. I told myself I couldn't object because I'd agreed to dine with him. And because I owed Neo Xenakis a few non-confrontational gestures.

Thinking he was leading me to the large, antique-filled dining room I'd spotted earlier during my brief and tentative search for the bathroom, I followed him in surprise into a kitchen fit for the world's most exacting chef.

Every imaginable gadget gleamed in polished splendour atop marble surfaces. On a large centre island, silverware gleamed under strategically suspended ceiling lights. Even the elevated stools looked too expensive for such a mundane activity as sitting.

But when he pulled one back and waited with tight expectancy, I swallowed the unnerving sensation that I was tangling with a supremely affluent and powerful man.

To the stout, rouge-faced chef who entered, I gave a quick smile. With a deferential nod, he started to uncover silver dishes.

Glorious smells hit my nostrils, and I stared at the mouth-watering array.

Exquisitely prepared Greek meze dishes were laid out next to an old-fashioned English shepherd's pie. I didn't fool myself into thinking this consideration had been made because I was joining him on such short notice. If the internet was right, Neo Xenakis was a man of extensive tastes and larger-than-life appetites.

Why that reminder triggered another wave of heat through my system I refused to consider as, with a few words, Neo Xenakis dismissed the chef and reached for the bottle of red wine that stood an arm's length away.

Seeing the label, I felt my eyes widen. Once upon a time, before he'd pulled the rug from beneath our feet with his stark betrayal, my father had been as much of a wine enthusiast as my mother was a magazine fanatic. When I was old enough to take an interest, he had often recited his dream vintage collection. The five-figure-price-tagged Château Cheval Neo cavalierly reached for now had ranked among the top three on my father's wish list.

I watched, slack jawed, as he deftly uncorked the bottle and set it aside to breathe.

Catching my expression, he narrowed his eyes. 'Something wrong?'

I swallowed. 'Nothing that doesn't involve my wondering if you normally share expensive bottles of wine with criminals before sending them to their doom.'

His gaze hooded, he shrugged. 'Satisfying your curiosity isn't on my agenda, so you'll just have to keep wondering. Eat.'

I toyed with refusing the order. But I was starving. And, really, he didn't *have* to feed me. With one quick call he could have Wendell tossing me out. Staying might grant me the opportunity to make another plea for mercy.

I placed two beautifully wrapped vine leaves onto my plate, then added a couple of spoonfuls of Greek salad. About to lift my fork, I paused when his eyes narrowed again, this time on my plate.

'You haven't eaten all day and that's all you're having?'

'Yes.'

He nodded at one of the many platters. 'The *kopanisti* won't keep. Don't let it go to waste.' He picked up serving tongs and caught up a dish of salad, roast peppers and an orange paste laid in between two crisp flatbreads. 'Try it,' he said.

Tentatively, I picked up the large morsel and bit into it. Sensations exploded in my mouth as the orange paste, which turned out to be the most incredible aged feta, combined with everything else immediately became the best thing I'd ever tasted—which in turn triggered a groan of appreciation before I could stop myself.

Perhaps my vivid imagination was playing tricks on me,

but I could have sworn Neo swallowed hard at that moment, and I felt his tension ramping up.

Abruptly, he spooned several more items onto my plate, then reached for the wine bottle. 'Would you like some wine?'

The chance to try the jaw-droppingly expensive vintage, especially considering that my fate hung in the balance, was too much to resist. 'Just a little, please.'

After pouring two glasses, he chose steamed white cod and a spoonful of salad himself, which he polished off with a military efficiency that spoke of fuel intake rather than enjoyment. Then he simply sat, slowly twirling the stem of his wine glass, lifting it occasionally to his lips as he watched me eat.

Self-conscious, and reluctant to broach the ultrasensitive subject of my crime, I stilled my tongue in favour of enjoying the most exquisite meal I'd had in a long time, all the while painfully aware that his gaze hadn't shifted from me.

'Which university?'

I started. 'What?'

'Your marketing degree,' he expounded.

I named it, and again caught the faintest hint of surprise in his eyes as he slotted the information away, his long fingers still twirling his glass.

'Do you like aeroplanes?' he asked abruptly, after another stretch of silence.

'Who doesn't?'

His lips tightened and his gaze dropped to my empty plate, then shifted to the platters of lamb cutlets, grilled meatballs, roasted vegetables and bread.

Sensing he was about to push more food on me, I sat back. 'That was delicious. Thank you.'

He frowned, then lifted the lid off a dish set apart from the main courses. The scent of spun sugar and warm pastry washed over me, almost eliciting another groan. I'd been cursed with a sweet tooth—one that needed constant attention.

'Dessert?' he offered gruffly, pushing the baklava directly in front of me.

The sight of the perfect little squares of delight was too much to resist. At my helpless nod, he placed four pieces on a fresh plate and slid it in front of me, again seemingly content to simply sit back and watch me eat.

Perhaps this was Neo Xenakis's method of torture. To feed me until I burst.

At that mildly hysterical thought, I let my gaze flick up to meet his. Again that spark flared in his eyes, and the charge seized me, causing tingles from my palms to my toes.

'If it wasn't for this wholly unfortunate situation, I'd think you didn't want me to leave,' I mused. Then immediately cursed my runaway tongue.

He froze, his grey eyes turning as turbulent as a lightning storm. His hand tightened around his glass, his fingers turning white.

'I'm sorry. I didn't mean—'

'Perhaps you're right,' he interrupted, his voice low, rough and raw, as if scrabbled from a pit of utter despair. 'Maybe I *don't* want you to leave. Maybe I need you sitting there in front of me as a reminder of what has happened. Of the fact that the nightmare you brought to my doorstep isn't one I can wake up from.'

The utter bleakness in his tone launched a lump into my throat. My fingers tightened in my lap as the need to reach out, to lay my hand on his or cup that rigid jaw, powered through me. I did neither, sensing it wouldn't be welcome.

'Is it really that hopeless? Is there no chance that things can be salvaged?' My question was a desperate one. But the thought that things could really be so dire for a man so incredibly masculine and virile looking seemed unthinkable to me.

'Excuse me?' he rasped icily, his eyes turning almost black with the strength of his emotions.

I pushed my plate away and forced myself to answer before I lost my nerve. 'I… Surely it doesn't surprise you that I'd wonder why a man who looks like you—'

'*Looks like me?*' he grated.

I wetted suddenly dry lips, suspecting I'd strayed into dangerous territory but unable to locate the road map to take me out of peril.

'You're not blind. You look like the poster-perfect image of virility. Is it beyond the realms of probability that I'd wonder why you'd need to use a facility like the Phoenix Clinic?'

His eyes slowly rose. 'Did you not admonish me for judging *you* based on your outward appearance?'

Even as my face heated, something inside me reacted sharply to the notion that I might have ended this man's line with my mistake. Something that utterly rejected that thought.

'Please answer the question, Mr Xenakis,' I urged, aware of my escalating desperation.

'Why? Are you distressed by the thought that a man who *"looks like me"* might be impotent or infertile?' he drawled.

He was goading me, pure and simple. I should've looked away. Backed down.

'Are you?'

He rose and stepped away from the island. 'Come with me,' he grated.

Something raw and intense pulsed in his tone, warning me that whatever he had in mind would decimate me emotionally.

'And if I refuse? Is this where you threaten—'

He slashed one powerful hand across my argument, his lips flattening into a displeased line. 'A word to the wise, Sadie. If you have any desire for self-preservation left in that body, be wise and stop defying me at every turn. I'm a man who faces adversity head-on. Right now, I'm *this* close to tossing you out the door and letting the authorities deal with your crimes. But, again, the choice is yours. Leave and face the consequences or indulge the man you've so gravely wronged. Which is it to be?' he asked, his eyes pinning me in place.

'I… Fine. I'll do what you want. For now,' I tagged on, simply because that self-preservation he'd mentioned was kicking in wildly, doubling my thundering heartbeat. 'I reserve the right to leave any time I want.'

He left the kitchen without responding.

I followed, striving not to breathe in his intoxicating scent and failing miserably.

Senses jumping, I watched him stroll over to the plush sectional sofa, sit down on it in a deceptively relaxed pose, one long arm lazily stretched out on the top of it. He rested one ankle on his knee, and lifted his wine glass to take a liberal sip.

'If you wish. But why postpone the inevitable? And why annoy me further by forcing me to carve another appointment into my schedule when we can settle this one way or the other tonight?'

Because I needed the headspace to think straight!

But Neo Xenakis would be equally imposing and breathtaking tomorrow—and most likely every day from now until eternity.

So why delay the inevitable indeed?

With legs turned rubbery, and nigh on useless, I approached him.

'Let me give you the broad strokes of the consequences of your actions. I come from a large family. Perhaps not your conventional Greek family, but we adore babies without reservation, regardless of how they were conceived,' he said, his hooded gaze on the contents of his glass. 'Which means that from a relatively young age, certain obligations have been required of me. Obligations I had every intention of fulfilling at some point in the future. Do you understand what that means?'

My nod was jerky at best. 'Something along the lines of keeping the family name going?'

'Exactly so. And I take my duty seriously. So what do you think you owe me for effectively ending my chances of fulfilling my obligations?'

'But…have I really?' I asked, unabashed curiosity getting the better of my tongue.

The turbulent emotion in his eyes receded for a moment, replaced by an equally arresting gleam as his gaze raked my face before resting with quiet ferocity on my mouth.

'I see we're back to that little nugget you can't let go of. Are you asking me if my equipment works, Sadie?' he drawled.

There was a layer of danger to his tone that should have frightened me but instead caused the blood to rush faster through my veins, pushing a flood of colour into my cheeks.

'I can't help thinking…it would help to know if the situation is as dire as all that…'

*God. Stop talking.*

'And if it isn't?' he rasped. 'Are you hoping that with one simple answer you'll be absolved of what you've done?'

God, we were really discussing his…his…

'No. Maybe. Yes…' I whispered.

'My ability or inability to engage in intercourse is not the issue here,' he said.

'Answer the question anyway,' I blurted, attempting to keep my mind on the important subject at hand and losing the battle in favour of racy thoughts of the exploration of his mouth-watering body first-hand.

Growing stupidly breathless, I scoured his face, his sculpted cheekbones, the hard angles of his jaw, the shadowed enticement of his strong throat and…dear God…the sensual curl of his lower lip, currently curved against his glass as he took another lazy sip.

The way he simply…lounged in his seat, was deceptively calm in a still-waters-run-deep manner. I wanted to dive into those waters, lose myself in them until I was completely sodden.

A different sort of heat pummelled me, low and insistent, charting a path of ravenous need directly between my thighs. Against the lace cups of my bra my nipples tightened, and each breath drew urgent attention to the decadent craving coursing through my body.

'I could tell you—but should I? I owe you nothing. You have no right to answers. But if you truly want to know if I can get it up, I invite you to find out for yourself,' he rasped thickly, his hooded gaze announcing that he knew every single yearning crashing through me.

My tongue thickened in my mouth, and that same acute urge to test where this alternative route would take me rammed unadulterated temptation through my bloodstream.

*Sweet heaven.* Surely he wasn't really suggesting what I thought he was…? And surely I wasn't truly considering it.

Was I?

# CHAPTER THREE

MY BREATH BURST from between my lips, the wild, dizzying leap of my pulse a damning testament to the fact that his words had exhilarated me for one blind nanosecond before reason reasserted itself.

*He can't truly mean that. He's just toying with you.*

Even if he wasn't, the proposal was absurd.

'Is this a joke?'

'Do I look amused, Sadie?' he returned.

No, he didn't. That raw confession in the kitchen returned, and the looming possible result of my actions—that I'd deprived not just him and his immediate family but the larger Xenakis clan of his future descendants—hit me with powerful force.

Helpless despair wove through me, and my chest tightened as I watched him, attempted to see beneath the taut mask of his face. Was this all because he truly didn't want to be alone to confront the dire position I'd put him in?

If so, was this his answer?

I shook my head. 'I… I'm not sure what this is all about.'

He shrugged. 'You want me to provide spoilers for a story you seem very interested in. I invite you to peek beneath the cover. Or are you all bluster?'

'Just so we're clear, I'm not making any so-called reparation in the form of sex,' I blurted. Simply because my imagination was threatening to take flight again, and the look in his eyes was sending my senses into free fall once more.

I grappled them down—hard.

One mocking eyebrow elevated. 'You jump to conclusions with the same careless abandon that I suspect landed you in this predicament in the first place. Perhaps you should wait until you're invited to my bed before you respond in one way or another.'

His censure smarted, regardless of the fact that I'd agreed to give him a little leeway in the perpetrator-versus-victim scenario.

'I'm not stupid, Mr Xenakis. I can read between the lines. And whatever you think is going to happen here, it isn't,' I stressed, although the caution was equally for me as it was for him.

'Has no one told you to quit while you're ahead?'

Many times. But I never went against my instinct.

'I believe in laying my cards on the table.'

Slowly, his relaxed stance altered. His arm dropped from the sofa, his body leaning closer as he pinned me with his gaze. With the width of the sofa between us, he wasn't crowding me. But he didn't need to. His presence filled every square inch of space, proclaiming his power and glory in ways that were hard to define and impossible to dismiss.

'Do you? Well, hear this. If I wanted you in my bed you would come—and willingly. Not because of the unfortunate circumstances you find yourself in.'

'If that's some sort of dare, I promise I won't be taking it,' I stated firmly, despite that insidious temptation striking deep. Deeper. Making my every breath strain, making my nipples tingle and peak and *yearn*.

God, what was wrong with me?

He shrugged again. Drawing my eager attention to the firm, bronzed expanse of his throat. Striking me with a fervent need to place my hand right there...where his pulse throbbed powerfully beneath his skin.

I averted my gaze, but the lingering look he gave me said he'd caught me staring. I needed to get up. Leave. Put some distance between myself and the turbulent temptation that *oozed* out of him. But doing so would send another weakening message. He'd invited me here. I'd lobbed the ball into his court. So I waited for his move.

The muted sound of a door opening heralded the arrival of a butler, bearing a silver tray with more drinks on it. While I was a little startled, Neo looked unruffled, as if nothing unusual had happened to interrupt his normal after-dinner routine.

He accepted a glass of cognac, then glanced at me. 'Nightcap?'

I shook my head, surprised at his cordial tone. Then I snapped my spine straight. I couldn't afford to lower my guard. He still hadn't spelled out the parameters of my reparation. Nor given me a straight answer to my question…

With a few words Neo dismissed the butler. The moment we were alone, he discarded his untouched drink and turned his piercing gaze on me.

My eyes connected with his as if pulled by invisible magnets. As much as I was reluctant to admit it, the man was a superb specimen. His impossibly broad shoulders demanded attention, and the gladiator-like synergy of sleekness and power combined with an animalistic aura impossible to dismiss.

The look in his eyes intensified, sending the distinct message that now we were getting down to the heart of whatever was on Neo Xenakis's mind.

'Come here, Sadie,' he ordered, confirming my frenzied thoughts.

*Get up. Walk out. He can't stop you.*

But temptation could. It wrapped its sinuous vines around me, hard and fast, left me breathless and speechless.

This was theory testing. Curiosity satisfying. Nothing else.

My life had taken a left turn this morning. Not that things had been rosy before… My mother and her gambling problem, my landlord's growing threats, my jobless state… My life and plans were a world removed from what I'd imagined for myself back in the idyllic days when I had the illusion of a solid family. When a fulfilling career, perhaps eventually a family, wasn't a laughable, ephemeral prospect.

The dismaying sensation in the pit of my stomach that had arrived along with my father's callously dismissive postcard and stayed all these years later, the sensation that mocked and questioned and poisoned my dreams, claimed I was as worthless as my father had deemed me, was very much present now, questioning my audacity to remain here, reaching for this temptation.

*Step back*, it said. *This isn't for you.*

But I wasn't ready to step back into my life just yet. I craved more time in this peculiar bubble with Neo Xenakis. Just for a little while longer.

Before I could stop the motion, I swayed towards him.

He didn't reach out. Simply lounged against the velvet seat, the king of his shiny castle, awaiting his due. And, like a moth to a flame, I couldn't resist the danger, the excitement, the *otherness* he offered.

One taste. Then I could end this any time I wanted.

One minute, then I could get back to why I was here, perhaps armed with the confirmation that he wasn't impaired in any obvious physical way.

The thought that I was attempting to slot this beneath the banner of *research* drew a hysterical chortle, quickly smothered beneath the pulses of lust swelling through my system.

Before I knew it, my body hovered next to his, almost horizontal on the sofa as I heeded his command.

'Here I am,' I replied in a voice that sounded nothing like mine.

Storm-tossed eyes traced every inch of my face, lingering longest and fiercest on my mouth.

'Yes. Here you are,' he replied.

His warm, cognac-tinged breath washed over my lips, causing them to tingle wildly.

Desperately, I slicked my tongue over them, then again when his sizzling gaze followed the wet path. His next breath emerged a touch harsher, his sculpted chest straining against his pristine shirt. The tingling flashed to my fingers, where the need to explore that mouth-watering expanse lashed harder and faster.

'The invitation still stands, Sadie,' he breathed.

Stay. Explore. *Indulge.*

I lifted my hand until it hovered mere inches from his skin. Until his heat caressed my palm, its gravitational pull tugging me with unrelenting force.

Was I really doing this? Baiting a predator to avoid my own reality?

Snatching a jagged breath, I hesitated.

Eyes even fiercer, Neo shifted. My hand met the hard wall of his chest, rested on the powerful thundering heartbeat. Lust burst through like a hot ray of sunshine through fog, melting away the last of my reservations. I slid my fingers up superbly well-defined pecs, over the tie he'd loosened during dinner, to glide around his neck.

The thought that I was headed in the wrong direction, going up when I should be heading down, evaporated as I explored him. He'd invited this. And I wanted to make sure my investigation was…*thorough.*

His eyes grew hooded when my fingers speared the hair at his nape. Lustrous strands slid through my fingers, and that small act fired up the tempest coursing through me. Enthralled by the sensation, I repeated the caress.

A gruff sound left his throat. His Adam's apple moved in a strong swallow. Had he moved closer or had I? My gaze fell to his full lower lip, so temptingly close. Promising a heady reprieve from chaos, despair and uncertainty.

One tiny, tiny taste.

I strained another inch closer, watched his eyes turn darker, felt his chest expand with a heavy inhalation.

One second ticked by. Two.

Then, with a rush of breath and a growl of impatience,

he breached the gap between us, fused his lips to mine in white-hot possession.

Indecent. *Heavenly.*

Outrageous and masculine and, oh, so powerful.

Neo took control of the kiss, brazenly swept his tongue along the ultrasensitive flesh of my bottom lip before delving in between to taste me. With a whimper of urgent need, I parted my lips wider, welcoming him with the eagerness of a starving woman granted a feast.

But even while his lips clung to mine, his hands remained where they were, maddeningly removed from my body. The challenge was too much to resist. Crawling closer, I wrapped both hands around his neck, drew him deeper into the kiss. Dared to meet his tongue with mine on the next sweep.

His body jerked and another growl left his throat as our tongues found a unique dance of decadent delight, of thrilling desire that built with each ferocious second.

Dear God, he could kiss. Even when he wasn't putting his complete effort into it, even when he wasn't touching me, I was nearly driven out of my mind.

In another heartbeat that was all I wanted. Neo Xenakis's hands on me.

Then I would stop.

Because this was getting out of control.

As if he'd heard my silent plea, he finally dropped his hands from the back of the sofa. They glided over my shoulders, down my ribcage, in slow, sensuous exploration to my waist. After the merest hesitation, he wrapped his large hands around my hips and pulled me with supreme masculine ease into his lap.

No need for any southern exploration.

The unmistakable evidence of his proud manhood was imprinted, hot and thick, against my bottom.

At my muted gasp he broke the kiss and edged me back, long enough to deliver a smouldering look of arrogant confirmation.

'Now you know,' he breathed.

'Y-yes…'

A look flickered through his eyes—one that seemed to ask and answer a question in the same heartbeat. Then he was tugging me back into his body, one hand spiked in my hair, the other on my hip, pinning me to his lower body. It was as if he wanted nothing but his powerful masculinity to occupy my mind now he'd provided the evidence.

As if I could think of anything else. *Feel* anything else.

With only one lover in my past, and a fleeting one at that, sex was still a mystery to me—a land whose borders I'd barely breached before retreating, first out of disappointment and then through the sheer strain of holding the tattered rags of my life together.

Now, presented with this tantalising feast, every past experience paled to nothing. My instinct warned that a man like Neo would have more experience in his little finger than I would in my whole body. That this brief taste was merely a drop in the ocean of what he could deliver to the right woman.

Except I wasn't the right woman.

I was the woman he'd goaded into taking this risky, mind-altering challenge. A challenge whose fire blazed to heights I'd never encountered before.

*You can stop. Now.*

But his lips were intoxicating. And the way his tongue and teeth and lips commanded mine was intensifying that persistent, needy throb between my legs…

With another moan I locked my hands around his neck, strained even closer to that magnificent body. And gasped when he abruptly pulled back, his hooded eyes darting from my parted lips to clash with mine.

He let out a heavy, unsteady exhale. 'This isn't how I foresaw this meeting evolving,' he rasped.

'Me neither,' I muttered.

He gave a short, jerky nod before his fierce gaze bored

into mine. 'Then perhaps it's best if we draw a line under it,' he invited.

But the slight clench of his fingers on my hip said that wasn't what he really wanted. And when his hold loosened, when I sensed he was about to disengage, I clenched my gut against the lash of disappointment and loss.

'Is that what you want? For me to leave?'

His jaw clenched and that hot gaze locked on my lips. 'The more important question is, are you ready to let go, Sadie? I ask this because you're clinging to me as if I'm the last piece of driftwood in your ocean.'

My arms unlocked from around his neck, slow with a helpless need to stay connected, moved down his chest. At his deep shudder a powerful sensation gripped me, along with a twinge of uncertainty barely born, before it was smashed beneath the colossal hunger clawing through me.

I'd never felt anything like this. And the voice inside telling me I never would again birthed a terrifying need to seize this unique experience.

Everything around me was slowly crumbling to dust. My mother's spiralling gambling. Looming homelessness. The job I no longer had. My own shattered dreams…

A secret fear plagued me in the dead of night. One I'd never admitted to anyone. That perhaps my father was right. That unconditional love was an illusion—an obligation fulfilled only up to a point. Or worse, that *I* hadn't been worthy of the effort.

The urgent need simply to forget for a little while longer hooked me with mighty talons, refusing to let go.

'Say what's on your mind,' Neo insisted.

The raw demand in his voice. The turbulent look in his eyes. The edgy hunger in his face. All of them echoed the deep clamouring inside me perfectly. Like two halves of a magnificent, earth-shaking whole. And really, in the desolate landscape of my uncertain future, where and when would I get the chance to experience anything close to this?

'Maybe I'm not…not ready to let go. Just yet.'

For the briefest moment he hesitated, as if he intended to refuse this…refuse *me*. More than a little panicked at the thought of being thrust back into my dreary life, I clung to his lapel.

Need smashed through his fleeting resistance.

Decadent headiness filled me, swirling in a sense of triumph I knew it was unwise to savour.

Strong fingers delved back into my hair, impatiently freeing the knot. As if he'd uncovered a wondrous sight, his breath caught as he fingered the long strands. 'Your hair is like a living flame,' he rasped, watching the thick tendrils glide over his skin.

The next instant he'd tugged open the button holding my jacket closed, pulled it off and had me back against the sofa, angling his powerful body over mine. I clung tighter to him, revelling in the erotic thrill of his kiss.

A moan ripped free from him as he settled his hips between mine and I felt the full power of his arousal. '*Theos mou*, you're intoxicating.'

And he was far from lacking in the ultimate manhood stakes.

I wanted to return the compliment, but words failed to form beneath the assault of his touch. His tongue boldly stroked mine, coaxed it into a thrilling dance, and all coherent thought evaporated.

We kissed until we grew breathless, only the need for oxygen driving us apart.

Frenzied seconds ticked away as Neo stared down at me. From unkempt hair to parted lips to strained nipples. There was nowhere to hide my attraction to this man—the last man I should've been doing this with.

Whether he felt the same or not became a non-issue as he resolutely levered himself away from me to shrug off his jacket. His tie followed, both tossed away with complete disregard for expense or care.

Hot hands slid around my hips once more, moulded them for an exploratory second before gliding downward, past my thighs and calves to my feet.

He removed and tossed away my shoes. Eyes locked on mine, he conducted the most maddening caress of one foot before digging an expert thumb into the arch.

A melting sensation pooled into my belly, a lusty moan leaving my lips.

For one fleeting moment, his lips twitched, as if he'd gleaned something about me that pleased him.

By the time he was done with paying the same attention to the other foot, my back was arching off the sofa, my whole body caught in waves of pleasure so unique I couldn't catch my breath.

He caught me in his arms, and sensation, earnest and powerful, overwhelmed me. Neo too, if his almost frenzied need to divest me of my clothing, filling the room with decadent sounds that escalated the passion-infused air, was any indication.

In minutes he'd reduced me to my panties and bra, and his hand was exploring every exposed dip and curve.

He lowered his head. At the thought that he was about to put his lips on my skin for the first time, I blindly reached for him, eager to undress him before I lost the ability to perform the function.

The first few buttons of his shirt came undone, giving me a tantalising glimpse of what lay beneath. But when I reached for the next one, Neo tensed, one hand staying mine.

'No,' he rasped, his voice tight.

Before I could question his response, he dropped his head and laid an open-mouthed kiss on the pulse racing at my throat, then counterpunched by grazing his teeth over the sensitive flesh.

'Oh!'

'You like that?'

'Yes!'

His satisfied growl set off cascades of shivers, rendering my nerve endings even more sensitive as he intensified his caress. One hand slid behind my knee, parting my legs so he could mould his lower body to mine, accentuating his lean hips and the powerful outline of his erection. I swallowed, momentarily apprehensive of his overwhelming maleness.

Pausing, his gaze bored into mine. 'Sadie, do you want this?'

The question was grave, and it also held a warning. He was reaching the end of his tether and he wanted to grant me the opportunity of ending this before insanity spun us completely out of control.

I didn't want it to end. I was on that same edge.

I boldly cupped his bristled jaw. He exhaled harshly, his sensual lips planting a hard kiss in my palm even while his eyes demanded an answer.

'Yes,' I replied.

Whatever regrets came later—and I suspected there would be many—I was too far gone, had given too many pieces of myself to heartache, from my father, worry over my mother, despair over life itself, to deny this unexpected slice of heaven. Even if it came in the form of an intense, larger-than-life man who was losing himself in me because of the colossal wrong I'd done him.

'I want this,' I confirmed, glad my voice held firm.

The words were barely out of my mouth when, with a deft flick, he released my bra. Eyes locked on mine, he dragged the straps down my arms. For a taut second after he flung it away, his eyes remained on mine. Then his gaze dropped to what he'd uncovered. A breath shuddered out of him.

'You're exquisite,' he breathed.

Pleasure arched my back, the act snatching his next breath. His head dropped, sensual lips wrapping around one peak to pull the tight bud into his mouth. I cried out as pleasure ripped through me, my senses scrambling further when his tongue swirled in erotic caresses. More decadent sounds fell from my lips. My fingers slid beneath the collar of his shirt to track urgently over his shoulders, to grip his back, eager to hold him to his task.

Neo's caresses grew bolder as he switched his attention to the twin peak. Arrows of need shot between my thighs, dampening and readying me for the ultimate possession. Possession he seemed determined to tease out as he feasted on my breasts for an age, returning over and over to my mouth to demand torrid kisses.

Just when I thought he'd drag the moment out for an eternity he drew down my panties, flinging them away with the same sexy carelessness he'd given my bra.

'I have to taste you,' he said, in that deep, raw voice, gripping my thigh to part me to his avid gaze.

His stare was so potent, so ravenous, I lost what little breath I had left in my lungs. 'Neo…'

'Shh, no talking, *glikia mou*. Quite enough words have passed between us.'

Denied that outlet, I grasped another. I touched, I explored, I kissed every covered muscle within reach, delighting in the slivers of heated olive skin he allowed me.

Right until his bold lips delivered the ultimate kiss between my thighs.

I fell back, boneless, onto the sofa, and another cry was wrenched from my throat as he wreaked wicked havoc between my thighs. All the while delivering rough praise in English and Greek.

How had I even contemplated denying myself this soul-stirring experience? Even at this stage, I knew it paled in comparison with my brief sexual foray back at uni.

Neo tongued my nerve-filled bud and I screamed, the shameless keening urging him into deeper caresses until it all grew too much. Until I had no choice but to surrender to the blistering release that gripped me tight for several electrifying seconds before tossing me into utter bliss.

For endless minutes I drifted, a raw mass of sensation.

But in excruciating increments I became aware of my surroundings, of my fingers clenched in his hair. Of the wide, plush sofa beneath me and the hot body slowly prowling up mine. Of the foil caught between his fingers as he eased back, unzipped his trousers and pulled them and his boxers down.

His shirt remained on, the tails covering the tops of his thighs. Eyes pinned to mine, he glided the condom on with that mask of hunger stamped on his face.

Unable to help myself, I dropped my gaze to his shaft. And again I experienced momentary panic at his sizeable thickness. But, as if he'd willed it away with the sheer force of his attraction, the worry receded as he reclaimed his place between my legs.

Nevertheless, I couldn't suppress my whimper at the first breach.

He froze, teeth gritted, as his turbulent gaze searched mine. 'Sadie…?'

Fear that he would stop, that this insulating little bubble would burst and I would be flung back into dreary reality, pushed me to blurt out, 'Don't stop. Please.'

For heart-stopping seconds he didn't move. Just stared at me with a mixture of edgy intensity and banked lust. Then, as if he didn't want to leave this bubble either, he thrust deep.

Pleasure rolled over me, dissipating the initial sting of his fullness. 'Yes…'

Relief washed over his face, immediately chased away by wickedly ferocious determination. Another thrust. His groan melded with my moan as he slid to the hilt.

'You shouldn't feel this incredible,' he grunted. 'But, *thee mou*, you do.'

His words triggered a weird kind of triumph—a fleeting but overwhelming pride that I was good enough for something, *worth* this moment of nirvana. I sank deeper into sensation, shuddering at the powerful emotions moving in my chest. Then in pure carnal bliss Neo rolled his hips, driving me further out of my mind.

'More. Please.'

A wicked pause, then he seized my arms, dragged them above my head. The movement drew my body taut, enlivening every inch of me with intense awareness as he splayed his fingers between mine and proceeded to give me far more than I'd ever imagined possible.

With every thrust, every glide of his lips over my skin, I was hurled closer to that intense spark I knew would ignite the most sacred bliss I'd ever known.

I wanted to rush it and slow it down at the same time.

I wanted to hold it in my palm and savour it even while I strained for complete annihilation with every cell in my body.

'Please…' I panted, unsure which path I yearned for more.

With a series of piston-fast, mind-melting strokes, the moment arrived. White-hot, searing, intense. I was catapulted into unadulterated bliss, eagerly surrendering to the power and might of it.

His head buried in my neck, Neo gave a muted shout, his body shuddering for endless moments in the throes of his own release.

After the frenzied pace of his possession time slowed to a crawl, as if the power of our jagged coming together, the intensity of the moment, needed reverse momentum to slow and steady it.

Heartbeats slowed. Pulses quieted. Like a powerful drug taking me under, lethargy stole over me. I closed my eyes and drifted, cloaked in a moment's peace before I had to face what had happened.

The moment arrived all too soon.

First came the loss of the searing palm-to-palm contact that had somehow heightened this experience from base act to something…*more*, followed by the complete withdrawal of body heat when Neo rose lithely from the sofa, triggering an acute self-consciousness of my naked state in contrast to his almost completely clothed form.

Then, with his thick curse uttered in Greek, but nevertheless unmistakable, I was wrenched from my insulated bubble.

The living room lights, which had provided seductive ambience during our furious coupling, suddenly blazed too bright, exposed too much, making me blink a few times before I focused on the man frozen in a half turn from me, a look of stark disbelief and something else that looked like furious self-loathing etched into his face.

'I… Is something wrong?' I cringed at my husky sex-hoarse tone.

Neo ploughed his fingers through his hair, turned and stalked down the hallway. Dread dripped torturous ice water down my spine. The frantic darting of my mind was locked in place for several long seconds before I jackknifed upward, my feet landing on the plush carpet as I tried to marshal my thoughts.

It took far too long to find and wrestle my tangled panties on. I was cursing my shaking hands and their inability to straighten my bra straps when brisk strides signalled Neo's return.

My disquiet intensifying, I glanced his way. He ignored me. I told myself to be glad, but my stomach churned harder, the regret I'd anticipated and almost accepted would arrive suspiciously light in place of the hurt and confusion swamping me.

His movements jerky, unlike the smooth, animalistic grace he'd exhibited earlier, he headed for the drinks cabinet, but at the last moment veered away and stopped before the glass wall.

Silence pulsed as he stared out, ferocious tension riding his shoulders.

I dragged my fingers through my hair, shoving it out of

the way in order to secure my bra, and hurriedly punched my fingers through the sleeves of my blouse. I was tugging the sides together when he turned.

If his eyes had been turbulent pools before, they were positively volcanic now. But that fury was aimed more at himself than at me. There seemed to be bewilderment, as if I was a puzzle he'd tried and failed to put together and now loathed himself for attempting.

He stared at me for another unsettling minute, his lips parted, his chest rising and falling as if he detested the very words he was about to utter.

'We have a problem,' he grated.

I was surprised he could speak at all, with his jaw locked so tight and the tendons in his neck standing out.

The feeling of unworthiness returned—harder, harsher. *Not good enough*, the insidious voice whispered. *Never good enough.*

I pushed it and my roiling emotions away for examination later. Much, much later.

'I can tell. Although I'm at a loss as to what it is.'

But even as the firm words tumbled from my lips, the cascade and echo of old hurts was deepening, intensifying.

'If you're about to tell me you regret what happened, please save your breath. We don't need to dissect it now or ever. I'll be out of your hair in a few minutes. You need never set eyes on me again if that's what you—'

'The condom broke.'

The words were delivered like a chilling death knell. I was glad I hadn't attempted to stand, because my legs would have failed me. I was aware that my jaw had sagged, that I probably made an unattractive sight, sitting there half-dressed, with my skirt askew and unzipped and my blouse wrinkled.

He confirmed it with a quick rake of his gaze and a harder clenching of his teeth. 'Get dressed, Sadie.'

I ignored the command for the simple reason that I

couldn't move, couldn't force my brain to stop repeating those three damning words on a loop.

'I... What?' I finally managed.

'Cover yourself,' he repeated tersely.

'Why? My nakedness didn't cause the condom to fail,' I flung back, and then compounded my words with a furious blush as his eyebrows hiked upward in flaying mockery.

I turned my back on him, a much more earth-shaking tremble seizing me as the ramifications landed home. While he'd listed everything I may have deprived him of, Neo hadn't definitely confirmed his inability to father children. So did I face a possible pregnancy on top of everything else?

Dear God...

*Motherhood?* When my own blueprint of childhood was so flawed?

Somehow, through sheer will to fight this battle on some-where-near-equal footing, I straightened my clothes, slid my feet into my shoes.

There was nothing I could do about my hair, what with the cheap band I'd used nowhere in sight and my refusal to dig around for it under Neo's heavy, brooding stare. So I took a deep breath, and turned around to face the conse-quences of yet another wrong turn.

# CHAPTER FOUR

MISTAKE.

Big, colossal mistake.

Disbelief, raw and searing, tunnelled deep, bedded down into my bones with unstoppable force until I had no choice but to acknowledge its presence. To accept that I'd simply compounded one problem with not one but two further mistakes.

For the first time in my life I wanted to find the nearest sand dune. Bury my head in it. But I couldn't.

Because there she stood, a flaming hot testament to the temptation I'd given in to when I should've walked away. Should have heeded my own agency to retreat and regroup instead of arrogantly imagining I could handle this—handle *her*—like a normal business challenge, to be ruthlessly and efficiently dismantled before moving on to the next problem.

The chaos she'd brought upon me wasn't a business problem or even a wider family problem, to be accommodated only so far until it could be slotted under *someone else's problem* when in reality it was deeply, straight-to-the-core *personal*.

It had needed addressing, sure. But only once I'd thought things through. Executed a solution with military precision, as I did with everything in my life.

Not losing myself in the very object of my misery. Not letting go of the reins of my sanity so thoroughly and completely that the world could've burned to the ground and I wouldn't have minded in the slightest if it meant I could continue to enjoy her silken warmth, the intoxicating clutch of her tight heat. To hear those spellbinding gasps and cries fall from her lips as she begged for more.

Acid seared my throat, flooded my mouth, bringing with

it a recollection of the only other time I'd let blind lust get the better of me.

An invitation to some faceless heiress's birthday party in Gstaad I'd almost refused—until a possible business opportunity had been thrown in to sweeten the invitation.

A big deal bagged, followed by a night of hedonistic revelry.

A mistaken conclusion that I'd found a worthy soulmate, even though I'd never truly believed in that sort of flighty fantasy.

When that illusion had seemed to hold true in the clear light of day, for weeks and months, I'd congratulated myself for a wise choice made even in the midst of frivolity and decadence.

A proposal in Neostros, before friends and family, an engagement party to trump them all, and I was all set to buck the Xenakis family trend of backstabbing and buckling underneath the smallest pressure.

Even when suspicions arose…even when I allowed Anneka to talk me into another visit to Gstaad and a reluctant turn on the black ski run ended with me being launched twenty feet into the air and descending via a jagged aspen tree…she hadn't bailed.

Unlike most, who barely remembered their trauma, mine still played out in excruciating detail. I heard her cries as she held my hand and urged me to hold on. And I held on, remaining alert right until the doctors were forced to put me in a medical coma. I embraced even that, knowing she would be waiting for me when I woke.

But those fervent wishes for me to hold on had been born not of love but of callous greed and an unconscionable disregard for loyalty and integrity.

She calculated every move, right up until my eyes opened—literally and figuratively—to the betrayal and falsehoods so deeply ingrained she wore them like a second skin. One she attempted to hide with tears and cajoling until she'd learned that she couldn't fool a Xenakis twice.

I'd made a vow never to be caught in another traitorous web ever again.

*Where was that vow an hour ago, Neo?*

I stifled a growl at the mocking inner voice. There'd been quite enough growling for one night. One *lifetime*. The cold calculation with which I should have approached this situation finally arrived.

I stared at Sadie Preston. Watched her fidget, like she did in my office.

Then slowly that chin went up, throwing the face I'd framed in my hands and caressed into alluring relief while those green eyes began to spark.

'Are you going to stand there glaring at me all night? Look, I know the news is upsetting—'

Harsh laughter barked out of me, startling her, but there was no help for it. 'You think this is merely *upsetting*? Do you not understand that there's no making this right? No glossing over this?'

'I was just—'

'Attempting to make me feel better? Urging me to look on the bright side? Is *that* what the episode on the sofa was all about?'

Raw colour flared in her cheeks but she dared another step closer, that temper I'd suspected bubbled just beneath the surface rising. 'How dare you belittle it?' she breathed, stunning me with her fierce tone. 'It wasn't just a sordid little episode to me.'

'Wasn't it? If I didn't know better, I'd think you actually *mean* that.'

Another less readable look flashed in her eyes. Lips that had tasted exquisite beneath mine firmed, holding in whatever response she'd intended to utter for several seconds before she shook her head and spoke anyway.

'I know there's nothing I can say or do to alter what's

happened. But I was actually talking about the…the incident with the condom, not what brought me here in the first place.'

*Christos*, the broken condom. Another intensely unwelcome first in a day of abysmal firsts that needed to be smashed out of existence.

*But then you wouldn't have met her.*

*Skatá!* What was wrong with me?

I'd hung on to her when I should have handed her over to the authorities within minutes of her confession. Now was I playing devil's advocate with *myself*?

Never crossing paths with Sadie Preston was a trade-off I could cheerfully accept—and that gritty little knot in my stomach that called it out for a white lie be damned.

So what if my digital little black book hadn't been used for the longest stretch since its inception, and she, with that mystifying allure of defiance and sexiness, would've been a prime addition to it had we met under different circumstances?

Facts were facts. And the simple fact remained: sending her packing should have been my first and only course.

'The accident with the condom is another consequence to deal with. But it should be a fairly straightforward matter. I'll start by assuring you that you have nothing to worry about health-wise.'

She arched one well-shaped eyebrow. 'And I'm to take your word for that? Because you're…*you*?'

The clear censure in her tone grated. 'That's your prerogative. But other than the fact that I abhor liars, a man in my position would be extremely foolish not to take the necessary precautions when it comes to every facet of his life. My last medical check returned a clean bill of health. You're the only woman I've slept with since.'

Her eyes widened a touch, questions glinting in their depths. 'And what about…?'

The inevitable question. I needed to answer and it burned

its way up my throat—a searing reminder of why my association with this woman should have ended many hours ago.

'I'm sorry, but I can't *not* ask, can I?' she muttered.

Her expression morphed into one I'd seen on too many
faces of friends and family members. Even those without
full knowledge of what had happened in that hospital room
deigned to pity me. It was why I'd banned my family from
discussing my accident.

'I don't need your pity, Miss Preston. Or whatever that
look on your face is supposed to signify. The simple truth
is, I cannot father children. The *why* doesn't concern you.
It's a proven reality—which makes your offer of a further
visit to your previous place of employment null. The only
thing I need from you right now is reciprocal reassurance
that I'm not at risk after this unfortunate mishap.'

Her expression snapped back to that mixture of fiery irritation, hurt and censure.

She wore her feelings so plainly. She would be an abysmal poker player. So why did I crave to keep staring, keep
attempting to read what else she felt within this chaos?

'I tell you this only for reassurance, in light of everything that's happened. Let's call it a courtesy.' She paused,
pursed her lips. 'I've had one relationship. It lasted five
months, while I was in my second year at uni, and I took
every necessary precaution. So you have nothing to fear
from me medically either,' she snapped.

A layer of tension released its grip on me, even while
questions multiplied in my brain. Questions I batted away
because, no, I most definitely did *not* care who that relationship had been with. Or why it had ended. These days not
being 'in a relationship' didn't mean a woman was celibate.
Did she belong to anyone now?

The urge to know was overpowering enough to force my
fists closed, to grit my teeth just so the question wouldn't
tumble out.

*Thee mou*, I was losing it.

Her eyes widened as she stared at me. Evidently, my poker face needed work too. She glanced away, her eyes lighting on the shabby little handbag resting on the entryway console table.

When she headed for it I remained where I stood, not trusting myself to approach her. But staying put didn't mean denying myself one final scrutiny of her body. Now that I'd tasted the passion and beauty beneath her tasteless clothes, my body wasn't in any mood to obey my commands to relegate Sadie Preston to the wasteland where she belonged. Instead, it tracked the supple shape of her calves and ankles, the tempting curve of her backside, the dip of her waist.

Her hair…

My fist clenched tighter. I'd never given much thought to a woman's hair before, except perhaps in the way it framed the overall package. I'd dated blondes, brunettes and everything in between without alighting on any specified preference.

Sadie's hair had trademarked its own siren call. One that had hooked into me, driving me to a new and dizzyingly dangerous edge.

'I suppose you want me to leave?'

I refocused on her face. She'd reclaimed her bag and slung it crossways over her slim torso, dragging my attention to her full breasts. I forced my gaze away from the perfect globes, crossed the living room to the front door to summon the lift.

A draining type of despair, a kind I'd never known before—not even when I stared into the heart of Anneka's cruel betrayal—sapped the dregs of my energy. I held it at bay with sheer willpower.

Barely.

'Neo…'

I pivoted to face her, renewed tension vibrating through to my very bones.

'I don't recall inviting you to use my first name. There's

nothing more to discuss. And, just so you're disabused of any lingering notions of attempting to make this right, let me lay it out for you. There's no way back from what you've done. Short of divine intervention and immaculate conception, you've effectively *ended* me, Sadie Preston. My last hope of ever becoming a father was that sample you destroyed. So I'm confident that you can get it through that stunning red head of yours that if I never see you again it will be too soon. Attempt any form of communication with me for any reason and this stay of execution I'm considering will be off the table and you'll be handed over to the authorities to answer for your crime. Is that understood?'

All colour drained from her face, but that stubborn chin remained high. *Defiant.*

'Perfectly. Goodbye, Mr Xenakis.'

*Nine weeks later*

'You shouldn't be going to work today, Sadie. You look even worse than you did yesterday. And you were out like a light when I looked in on you before I went to bed. I didn't disturb you because I thought a full night's sleep would do you good, but I can see it didn't.'

I busied myself fetching milk I didn't need from the fridge to make a cup of coffee I didn't intend to drink. All so I could avoid my mother's gaze and the questions lurking therein.

Despite despair and bone-tiredness leaching the strength from my bones, I strove to remain upbeat. 'I can't afford not to go to work. And I'm fine, Mum.' The *I promise* I usually tagged on to the reassurance stuck in my throat. I couldn't promise anything. Because I *wasn't* fine.

I hadn't thought it possible to be this far from fine when I blinked back tears as Neo Xenakis's lift hurled me down to the ground floor after that unforgettable night.

I'd been wrong.

That cloying sense of unworthiness, germinated after my father's desertion and watered by doubts and hopelessness, had trebled overnight, and the enormity of what I'd done both before and after meeting Neo Xenakis had thrown me into a state of raw despair. One that'd grown exponentially with the final notice from our landlord a week ago.

We were on a countdown clock to homelessness.

I hadn't been able to bring myself to tell my mother yet.

But I'd been doing a lot of evading lately.

In between sporadic temping I'd ignored the flulike symptoms leaching my energy, initially attributing my delayed period to the condition. Even after a second period was a no-show, I'd refused to believe that fate would be so brutal. That the unthinkable could truly happen.

Then had come the bracing, inevitable acceptance that I wasn't the victim of lingering flu, or a stomach bug that only attacked in the morning, but that, yes, I *was* capable of conceiving immaculately.

Shock.

Disbelief.

A brief spurt of searing anger at Neo Xenakis and his lies.

Followed by that ever-present tug of despair. That feeling of unworthiness. That cruel little reminder that my own blueprint was flawed.

But even while despair lodged a heavy stone in my chest there also came a quiet, even more bewildering...*elation*. Even though I was twenty-five, working jobs that paid a pittance and on the brink of homelessness with a mother who'd promised me, when I finally broke down and begged her to seek help, to combat her growing gambling addiction but had since regressed—as evidenced by the online betting pages I'd spotted on her phone yesterday.

That crushing list of failings was what had overwhelmed me last night. Made me pretend to be asleep when my mother entered the bedroom we shared.

Elation should be the farthest emotion on my reality spectrum.

A hysterical thought flitted across my mind. Perhaps I should have taken a gamble on myself. I'd be wildly wealthy and down one less problem by now. Because, despite all the odds against it, I'd fallen pregnant with Neo Xenakis's baby after one utterly misguided folly.

*A baby…*

Sweet heaven…

*I can't father children…*

The lie had dripped so smoothly, so convincingly from his lips. And I'd *believed* him. Had even hurt for him. When all he'd been doing was cruelly toying with my emotions.

Had he seen my feverish desire to stay anchored, *connected*, for just a little while, and viciously exploited it as some sort of payback? Did the man I'd given myself to, in an act I suspected had involved more than just the physical, bear traits of the father who'd so callously rejected me…?

'Sadie, dear, are you sure you're all right? You've gone as white as a ghost.'

I swallowed the encroaching nausea and a bubble of lurking panic, thankful that my mother hadn't noticed that on top of my pseudo-flu I was also plagued by bouts of vomiting.

'I'm not sick, Mum. Really,' I said, infusing as much warmth into my voice as possible.

'Okay, well…if you're sure. I'm going back to bed. Have a good day at work.'

She left the kitchen after sliding a comforting hand down my back. Absurdly, the gesture made my eyes prickle.

I blinked the tears away, forced myself to revisit the subject that filled me with equal parts anger and dread: relaying the news to Neo.

His last tersely worded warning before tossing me out of his penthouse still lingered, two months on. And I believed he'd meant what he'd said.

*Then*, of course.

But in light of this life-changing news…

I wouldn't know until I tried. *Again.*

My initial attempts to contact Neo had met a brick wall, with a few snooty receptionists even threatening to block my number if I kept trying to reach their illustrious boss. Apparently Neo had issued word that I was persona non grata.

Initially aggrieved by the realisation, I'd stopped trying to reach him for all of three days, before accepting that this reality wasn't going to go away.

Neo needed to learn of his child's existence sooner rather than later. And answer a few pointed questions in the process…

Since returning to his building and risking arrest or worse was out of the question, I ventured onto social media—only to discover that the Xenakis family were embroiled in the kind of publicity that drove the tabloids wild.

Apparently, in the last few weeks, Neo's older brother Axios had returned from a brief trip abroad with his young wife in tow. A wife whose previous absence had been highly conspicuous, fuelling all kinds of scandalous speculation.

Now, not only had the young Mrs Xenakis returned from her mysterious absence without explanation, she'd apparently given birth while she was away. The reunited family had asked for privacy, but already several shots of a baby boy, Andreos Xenakis, had been leaked to the media. He was a gorgeous baby, who bore all the strong characteristics of possessing the Xenakis DNA.

How was Neo taking the news? And, the more important question, how would he take *my* news?

It was only eight o'clock. My temp job didn't start until ten. That gave me a little time to attempt to reach Neo again.

Distaste at the thought of stalking him online lingered as I powered up my laptop. The first headline I found made my stomach drop.

*Xenakis Aeronautics Soars to New Heights in the Far East.*

Exhaling shakily, I read the article, calming down when I saw it focused mostly on Axios Xenakis and his spearheading of the airline conglomerate's global expansion. Neo would be taking over the European arm of the company, starting with relocating to Athens with immediate effect.

The article was two weeks old. Which meant Neo might now be even further out of reach.

Suppressing the strong bite of despondency, I scribbled down the numbers of the Athens office, shut down the laptop and rushed to the bathroom just in time to heave.

A quick shower and a judiciously nibbled slice of dry toast later, I picked up my bag and headed for the door—only to pause when my mother called out.

'Oh, Sadie, when you can, do you think you can buy me some data for my phone? I seem to have run out.'

Desolation deadened my feet. The urge to tell her that I was barely holding it together emotionally and financially, never mind providing a conduit for her addiction, tripped on the edge of my tongue. But I was woefully ill-equipped for a replay of the inevitable tears and depression that had dogged Martha Preston's life since her husband's cruel desertion. As much as I wanted to dish out tough love, I could barely hold myself together, and nor could I afford to lose another job because I was late.

Vowing to tackle the subject again that evening, I shut the door behind me.

The morning trundled by in the tedium of filing and answering phones.

After using the first minutes of my late lunch break to calm my nerves, I dialled the number I'd saved.

One minute later I hung up, my ears ringing after a crisp, accented voice informed me that while Mr Xenakis was

indeed at his office in Athens, he did not accept unsolic-
ited calls.

No amount of pleading had shifted the receptionist's
stance.

In the middle of the busy London park, I gritted my teeth
and resisted the urge to scream. Or dissolve into helpless
tears. Instead, on a desperate urge, I called up the web page
of a budget airline, my heart racing when I saw a same-day
return flight to Athens.

It would put further strain on my tight bank balance, and
would require even more ruthless financial rationing, but
the temp agency had no placement for me tomorrow and I
had nothing planned for the weekend besides tormenting
myself with the many ways my failed childhood might af-
fect my baby…

Without stopping to debate the wisdom of it, I booked
the ticket.

Regardless of his reasons for stating a blatant untruth, I
owed Neo the news that he was going to be a father. Just as
he'd deserved to know of my mistake at the Phoenix Clinic.

Would he think it was another unforgivable mistake?

Would he walk away even sooner than my father had?

It didn't matter.

*No. It matters. It's why you won't stop shaking.*

I smothered the voice, shrugging mentally. For good or
ill, I was going to beard the formidable lion that was Neo
Xenakis in his den one more time.

But this time, I was suitably armed with what to expect.

The seat of the Xenakis airline empire was housed in a
sprawling ten-storey building that took up a whole city block
in the centre of Athens. Security was twice as tight as in
London, but this time I didn't linger outside. The brief,
succinct note I'd hastily written in the taxi ride and shoved
into an envelope trembled in my hand as I approached the
ultramodern reception desk.

Before the efficient-looking receptionist could voice the
disdain lurking in her eyes, I held out the envelope. 'It's essential that Mr Xenakis sees this immediately.'

Whatever expression she read on my face halted her answer. Rising, she took the note and walked away.

I retreated to the nearest set of expensive club chairs, arranged to maximise the appreciation of the stunning mar-
ble-floored, three-storey atrium that formed the welcoming
entry into the world of Xenakis Aeronautics, the words of
the note echoing in my head:

> *Mr Xenakis,*
> *I'm downstairs in your lobby.*
> *It's in your interest to give me ten minutes of your*
> *time.*
> *I'm certain you'll regret it if you don't.*
> *Sadie*

Bold words, which would either grant me an audience or
fritter away the mercy he'd shown me by not asking Wendell
to break out the handcuffs that day in London.

I looked up to see Wendell heading my way, as if summoned by my thought. My heart dropped, but I refused to
look away.

'If you're here to throw me out, you should know that
I'll simply turn around and come straight back. Maybe you
should tell your boss that?'

His expression didn't change. 'Mr Xenakis will see you
now.'

I swallowed my surprise and followed him.

This time, knowing the calibre of the man who waited
behind another set of imposing doors, I tightened my gut,
sure I could mitigate the effect.

I was wrong.

Being on his home turf had heaped another layer of magnificent appeal upon a man who already held more than his

fair share. In the sunlight that filtered through wide, rect-angular windows, his dark hair gleamed. A skin-skimming stubble highlighted his strong jaw, and with that sexy dim-ple in his chin it was impossible to stop the flare of heat that attacked my body, robbing me of vital breath for pre-cious seconds.

The matching jacket to his tailored grey trousers hung on a hook in the far corner of his office, leaving him in a pristine white shirt that moulded his broad shoulders and powerful biceps.

Terrified I was already losing the fight for composure, I hurried to speak. To get this over with.

'Thank you for seeing me, Mr Xenakis.'

Eyes that had been conducting a slow, thorough scru-tiny of me rose to fix on my face. 'Miss Preston.' His voice was grave. 'I'm beginning to think you have some sort of death wish. Or do you simply relish testing my patience?'

'Neither. Believe me, this is the last place I want to be.'

His arrogant head cocked. 'I sense the inevitable *but* coming,' he drawled mockingly. 'Although I have no earthly idea what it could be.'

Despite his words, he narrowed his eyes, as if he fully suspected a scam. Or worse.

*Say it. Just say it and leave.*

I sucked in a breath that went nowhere near replenishing my lungs or giving me the courage I craved. 'I'm pregnant. The baby is yours. I thought you should know.'

Deathly silence echoed in the vast office. Then he in-haled sharply, the white-hot sound sizzling across the large room.

'*Christos*, you *do* have a death wish,' he breathed in siz-zling disbelief, and his face, unlike last time, when there'd been shock and bleak despair, was a picture of complete and utter fury.

'I don't, I assure you. But—'

'Then you've taken complete leave of your senses. Be-

cause that can be the only viable explanation for this—'
He stopped abruptly, his hands clenching and unclenching at his sides.

For one mad moment I wanted to say yes. That only a peculiar strain of madness would explain why I couldn't look away from his face, why I couldn't quite catch my breath in his presence.

'The door is behind you. Use it right now or I won't be held responsible for my actions.'

It was a hushed entreaty, perhaps even a final attempt at civility for a man hanging by a thread.

Considering I'd jumped on a plane with little hope of being granted even this audience, I was surprised I'd got this far. But complete dismissal wasn't what I'd expected.

The urge to linger, to make him believe, if only for the sake of telling my baby someday that I'd tried, fired through me—along with the question that still demanded an answer. The question about his false statement, the consequences of which had certainly taken *me* by surprise.

But Neo's face was turning even more ashen, his chest rising and falling in rapid shudders as he remained frozen in place.

'Why?' The question was ragged, torn from his soul.

'Excuse me?'

He prowled forward several steps, granting me a better look at his face. And there it was. That look of desolation.

'Why would you do this? Did someone put you up to it? As a joke, perhaps?' he asked from between whitened lips. 'Or a bet?'

'We don't move in the same circles, Mr Xenakis. Nor am I friendly with anyone who would deliberately cause someone distress with such a prank.'

'Then tell me *why*?'

There was a tinge of desperation in his question. Of bewilderment.

'Because it's the truth!'

He jerked forward again, his throat moving as his eyes drilled into me. 'No, it's not. As I told you in London, I'm incapable of fathering children. Three years ago the best doctors in the world delivered that staggering news. And do you know what I did?'

Numb, I shook my head, my anger at his lies dissipating in the face of the searing emotion in his eyes.

'I found a set of doctors with better credentials than the original set. Guess what? They arrived at the same conclusion. So now do you see how what you're saying is impossible?'

*Why?*

*Where?*

*How?*

Questions flashed through my brain even while I accepted that this wasn't the time or place.

I licked lips gone dry with growing anxiety. 'I can't speak to your experience. All I can tell you is my truth.'

If anything, his fury grew. 'Does this *truth* involve a lapsed memory on your part?'

I shook my head. 'I'm sorry—you've lost me.'

His jaw turned to steel. 'You wouldn't be the first woman to find herself in this situation and devise a plan to pass another man's child off as—'

'Don't you *dare* finish that sentence!'

'Because it's much closer to this "truth" you seek to ram down my throat?'

'Because it's most definitely guaranteed to get you slapped! And while we're throwing accusations around, what about what you said to me?'

'I beg your pardon?'

'You assured me I had nothing to worry about. You said I couldn't get pregnant! That it was impossible.'

'And I have a file of medical reports to back that up. What do *you* have?' he snarled.

'I have that immaculate conception you wished for, apparently. Because three pregnancy tests last week and a trip to the doctor confirms that I'm carrying a baby. *Your* baby!'

He shook his head, started to speak.

I held up my hand. 'It's fine if you don't want to believe me. I don't care.'

'You *do* care or you wouldn't be here. Or be crying,' he grated.

Belatedly, I registered the dampness on my cheek. Hating myself for that weakness, I dashed my hand across my cheek. Only to feel more tears spilling.

'It must be a side effect of being repeatedly labelled a liar. Or... I don't know... Pregnancy hormones. But, no matter what, this was the right thing to do. And now it's done.'

*There—you've said your piece. Now leave.*

But my feet refused to move.

His eyes narrowed with laser focus. 'If there truly is a baby, does the news distress you that much?'

'*Yes!* You lulled me into a false sense of security, made me think I had the flu when I'm *pregnant*!'

He went a little pale, his movements jerky as he closed the gap between us. 'And what would you have done if I'd told you two months ago that there *was* this possibility, hmm? Considered your options *without* me in the picture, perhaps?'

'Watch your tone, Mr Xenakis. The last thing you should be doing is lounging on that lofty perch and looking down your nose at me. What happened between us was consensual. What happened with the condom was unfortunate. You do *not* have the right to question my character. Considering the way we parted, do you really think I would be here, right now, if that was my intention?'

He seemed lost for words even as his gaze scoured my face, dissecting my words.

'You said yourself you only verified the pregnancy a week ago. That means you're about two months along. It's not too late for other options. Maybe that's your plan? To leverage those options?'

His insult sank in, sharp as a stiletto blade. 'God, you can't help yourself, can you?' I realised I'd screamed the words only after they came out.

He frowned. 'Calm yourself, Sadie.'

'If you want me to calm down, then stop upsetting me— *Neo*!'

He sucked in a deep breath, then another. Then he whirled around, dragging his fingers through his hair. Swift strides put the width of the room between us and I watched him stare out of the window at the Friday afternoon traffic, tension riding his shoulders.

Walking out through the door should've been easy, but again that stubborn need to have him believe me held me rooted to the spot.

So when he abruptly grated, 'Perhaps we should discuss this further. Take a seat. Please,' I glared at his back for all of half a second before stumbling over to one of the twin plush sofas positioned tastefully at one side of his office.

Unlike his stunning but impersonal London penthouse, there were more signs of Neo Xenakis's personality here. Priceless objets d'art were placed next to pictures of what looked like his family, and there was even a framed child's drawing. On the coffee table, a large book on Mayan history was open to a well-thumbed page, and several more Aztec-themed books were piled to one side.

The notion that in another time or place I'd have liked to get to know this stranger whose baby I carried hit me hard.

I was busy pushing the thought away when I heard his deep, low tones. He stood at his desk, speaking in rapid-fire Greek. Done, he returned to the window and stood there for an age.

When he turned around, every inch of his body brimmed with purpose. 'You mentioned that you saw a doctor?'

'Yes…after I took the pregnancy tests.'

'And?'

'Everything's fine so far.'

'This probably won't come as a surprise to you, but to me the possibility of an offspring is not…unwelcome.'

The depth of yearning in his low, deep voice rocked me to my core, softening a knotted place inside me I hadn't registered until his words loosened it. Truth be told, I hadn't allowed myself to think beyond delivering the news. Because when it came down to it, Neo had plenty of other options beyond having a baby with the woman who'd brought chaos into his life. If he was willing to accept—

'If it's mine, that is. And at this point I'm hard-pressed to be convinced it is.'

The soft place hardened, strangled tight by his words. 'You really believe I'd lie about something like this?'

The yearning receded slowly, forced back by the power of his scepticism. And something else. Something dark and grave that took complete control of him, hardening his face into a rigid, implacable mask.

'I'm a wealthy, influential man. Anyone with a competent internet connection can see for themselves what any association with the Xenakis family represents. Believe it or not, you won't be the first woman to attempt to saddle me with a paternity claim. Even when the likelihood is remote.'

He believed it. He truly believed he was infertile.

Despite the anguish dredging through me, a tiny voice urged reason. Urged me to see this from his point of view. How many headlines had I caught from my mother's gossip magazines that shouted about a celebrity vehemently denying alleged paternity? How many women had attempted to scam rich men by dangling a baby in their faces?

I was wasting my time.

Neo wouldn't believe even if I shouted until I was blue in the face.

I rose. 'Your hang-ups are your problem, not mine. I have a plane to catch, so I guess it's goodbye, Mr Xenakis.'

He moved with impressive speed. Before I could take my next breath, Neo had arrived before me.

'That's it? You came to deliver the news and now you're just going to head to the airport and return home?'

I dredged up a smile. 'Let me guess. This is where you expect me to make some sort of demand? Maybe ask for financial support or a McMansion to live in while I carry your child? Well, sorry to disappoint you. I want nothing from you.'

The faint colour tingeing his sculpted cheekbones told me I'd hit the nail on the head.

'Did you not hear me when I said I want this baby?' he asked.

'No, what I heard was you hedging your bets on the off-chance that I'm telling the truth. When you decide whether you want to believe me, I'm sure Wendell will be able to find me—'

'No,' he interrupted. 'That is most definitely *not* how this is going to work.'

'What's that supposed to—'

We both froze when déjà vu arrived in the hideously embarrassing form of my stomach giving the loudest growl known to humanity.

He muttered what sounded like an incredulous Greek oath under his breath. 'Tell me you haven't been neglecting to eat?' he bit out.

Heat consumed my face. 'I'm in the throes of a spectacular experience called morning sickness. Anything I eat before a certain time rarely stays down.'

He frowned. 'Surely there's a remedy for that?'

I shrugged. 'If there is, they haven't found it yet.'

His frown intensified. 'So the answer is what…? To starve yourself?'

'I don't do it deliberately, you know. My flight here was at an ungodly hour this morning.'

An exasperated puff of air left his lips as he glanced at

his watch. 'It's now past noon. Does this mean you haven't eaten all day?'

'I tried to eat something on the plane.'

His lips twisted in distaste. 'Budget airline food?'

'We can't *all* afford to travel on private jets, Mr Xenakis.'

'Neo,' he drawled. 'Call me Neo.'

'I'm not sure I want to call you anything, to be honest.'

'If the child you carry is truly mine there's one title you won't be able to deny me,' he stated with stone-rough gravity, just as a discreet knock sounded on the door.

He responded in Greek, and a moment later an impeccably dressed middle-aged woman entered, holding a package which she handed to Neo. Without glancing my way, she discreetly retreated.

He studied me for a moment, then reached into the bag. Although I suspected what the contents were, I was still shocked when he took out the oblong package.

'You sent out for a pregnancy test?'

'With the full intention of accepting any offence it might cause you, yes,' he stated simply, his fingers tight around the box. 'Will you take the test?' he asked, his tone containing a peculiar note I couldn't fathom.

There was something going on here. Something beneath the surface that I couldn't quite put my finger on. Again, questions surrounding the reasons why he believed he couldn't father children crowded my brain.

Resolutely, I pushed them away and accepted the status quo. For now. 'Only to prove I'm not a liar.'

I held my hand out for it but he hesitated, his jaw working for several seconds before he said, 'You should know that this is merely a preliminary test to confirm your pregnancy. A test for paternity will be necessary when the time is right.'

My hand dropped, something hot and sharp lancing my chest. 'You really are something else—you know that?'

'*Ne*, I've been told.' His stance didn't change.

'If you think I'm going to harm my baby just so your suspicions can be satisfied, you can think again.'

Emotion, heavy and profound and almost sacred, gleamed in his eyes. 'So you've made up your mind? You intend to keep it?' he rasped, his voice shaken.

'You think I flew three and a half hours on a cramped middle seat, next to a passenger with a rabid aversion to good personal hygiene, to tell you I'm pregnant, only to go back and get rid of it?'

Neo's gaze dropped to the hand I'd unconsciously jerked up to cradle my still-flat stomach.

'You think I don't have other things to do? I have a life to be getting on with. A mother who needs me to take care of—' I shut my mouth, but it was too late.

The moment his eyes narrowed I knew he was about to pounce on my unguarded revelation. 'Your mother needs taking care of? What's wrong with her?' he demanded sharply.

'It's none of your business.'

'I beg to differ. If this baby is mine—'

I swatted the rest of his words away. 'Enough with the *if*s. Here—hand it over. I'll take your precious test.'

Grim-faced, he held out the pregnancy test. I took it, then followed the tall, imposing body that hadn't diminished one iota in the drop-dead-gorgeous stakes in the last two months down a wide private hallway adjoining his office to a sleek, dark door.

The bathroom was another stylish masterpiece—naturally. Gleaming surfaces held exclusive toiletries, polished floors echoed my nervous tread and the wide mirror faithfully reflected my wan features.

I diverted my face from it, hurried into the cubicle and took the test.

A little over three minutes later, I stepped out.

He stood, square and true, five feet from the door, his gaze piercingly intent on the stick in my hand. For a single moment—knowing what this meant even if he doubted me, knowing I was perhaps about to change Neo Xenakis's life—something moved in my chest.

Then he ruined it by holding out an imperious hand for the test.

I handed it over.

His gaze dropped to it and he swallowed hard.

He seemed to rock on his feet—a fascinating feat to watch, especially for a toweringly powerful man like him. He didn't speak, only held the stick as if it was a magic wand that had the potential to deliver his most heartfelt wish.

Afraid I would succumb to softening emotions again, I hurried to speak. 'As you can see, it indicates how many weeks along I am. I can give you the date of my last period too, if you want?'

It was meant to be sarcastic. It fell far short simply because I wanted him to believe me. Wanted to take away his doubt once and for all.

Because I wanted to hurry to the part where, despite the evidence, he'd conclude that fatherhood wasn't for him after all. That this was a mistake. That *I* wasn't worthy to carry his child.

He didn't respond immediately. When he lifted his gaze his eyes were a stormy, dark grey, the pupils almost black. 'This is sufficient for now,' he finally said, his voice gravel rough.

Then he turned and walked away.

# CHAPTER FIVE

I COULD BARELY walk beneath the staggering evidence of what I held in my hand.

Confirmation that there was a child, possibly *my* child, shook through me with every step back to my office. The circumstances astounded me. Seemed almost too good to be true—the stuff of big-screen melodramas.

Had the woman who'd brought desolation to my door returned with redemption, despite my threat to her the last time she'd been in my presence? Despite the medical evidence I'd been provided with to the contrary?

What were the chances of lightning striking twice? Was I setting myself up for the same kind of betrayal Anneka had dished out so callously?

My jaw gritted, my stomach churning with the need for one hundred percent certainty.

I sucked in a calming breath, recalling what rash decisions had led me here in the first place. My fingers tightened around the stick. Not that I regretted it...*if* it was truly happening.

A bolt of euphoria threatened to overwhelm my calm. Brutally, I suppressed it. Rationalised it.

As Sadie had pointed out, the kit I'd asked my trustworthy assistant to purchase was the highest quality, giving an estimation of gestation. The test announced Sadie was more than three weeks pregnant.

Surely she knew how powerful I was? Knew that any information provided could be easily verified by my security team? Would she be so foolish as to toss out falsities that could catch her out?

A throat was cleared huskily behind me, making me aware I'd reached my desk, opened the secure thumbprint-accessed drawer that held confidential documents and was in the process of dropping the stick into it. I needed that connection, this visual evidence that maybe, just *maybe*, I'd defied science and the odds.

Again, stunned awe shook through me. A child. *My child.* But just as swiftly, a less effervescent emotion rose. A little desperate, and a lot dismaying.

The thought struck me that I had no true compass as to how to *be* a father. I'd gone straight from boarding school to boardroom, my spare moments spent watching my grandfather struggle to hang on to the company, and subsequently witnessed my father and Ax embroiled in a cold battle for the helm of the company.

I'd used my time on the sidelines efficiently—learned everything I needed to excel in my field.

*Those lessons hadn't included how to be a father.*

'Now that we've established that there's a pregnancy, are we done here?' she asked.

*Done here?* Was she joking? 'No, we're not done. Far from it.'

'What's that supposed to mean?'

'It means I intend to be involved in this baby's welfare every step of the way. Beginning now.'

I forestalled the questions brimming in her eyes by making a quick phone call.

The moment I was done, she approached.

Shock born of the earth-shattering news she'd delivered had partly blocked off the stunning effect of her appearance. Now, with the flood dammed and a plan of action swiftly slotting into place in order to secure what she insisted was mine, I couldn't stem my reaction to her.

The white sundress was a cheap and simple design, but on her it looked anything but. The scooped neckline gave a tantalising glimpse of the perfect breasts that seemed to have swelled a size bigger with her pregnancy. And her skin, now her temper had subsided, glowed with an additional translucence that triggered wild tingles in my fingers with a need to trace, to caress... *Christos*, to lay my lips against that pulse before stealing another taste of those rosebud lips, currently caught between her teeth as she watched me.

I bit back a growl as my gaze rose to that final monument to her beauty. Two months on, her hair had grown longer, the ponytail she'd caught the heavy tresses into almost down to the middle of her back.

The hunger to set it free, to lose myself in the exotic scent of it, powered through me.

'Explain what that means. Precisely. Because less than twenty minutes ago you were almost apoplectic about my perceived deception.'

I forced myself to throttle back this insane arousal that fired up only with her.

It wasn't for lack of trying that I'd remained dateless since that night in London. Hell, I might even have cursed Sadie Preston a little for the sudden urge to set my useless little black book on fire because not a single woman listed within sparked the kind of flame she did with a mere look.

'You have to be aware that I intend to take every precaution with you?'

Her wary glance confirmed that notion was becoming clear to her.

'I've told you I only came here to give you the news—which I could've done by phone if you hadn't blacklisted me.'

While the accusation grated a little, I couldn't allow it to dissuade me from forging ahead. 'From this moment forward consider that status reversed. You will have access to me day or night.'

Curiously, her breath caught, and I glimpsed something that looked like excitement in her eyes—which, perversely, triggered a stronger chain reaction within me.

Her trite reply attempted to disguise her reaction. 'Others might find that offer beyond tantalising, but I don't think much communication between us will be necessary after today...'

Unbidden, my lips twisted in genuine amusement, causing her words to trail off.

'I fail to see what's funny.'

Wonder. Apprehension. Raw anticipation. Panic. The cascade of emotions was threatening to send me off balance.

'You're carrying my child, Sadie. A Xenakis.'

Her eyes widened. 'So you believe the baby is yours?'

Betrayal's curse bit hard—a timely reminder to exercise caution. But for now I needed to buy myself time. After the accusations I'd hurled at her, and her reaction, these negotiations needed to be handled carefully while still keeping her under scrutiny. Because I didn't intend for history to repeat itself.

'In utero paternity tests carry unacceptable risks. We will wait until the baby is born.'

'And how do you know that?'

I clenched my gut against the searing reminder of how wrong I'd been before, how blind trust had almost decimated me.

'That doesn't matter. What matters is that we're in agreement that the health of this baby is the priority.'

She frowned. 'I don't need you to tell me that.'

'Then you'll stay a little while longer? Have lunch with me?'

Her eyes widened, then grew suspicious. 'Why?'

'You need to eat, do you not?'

Memory darkened her eyes and swept the most becoming blush across her skin. She was recalling what had happened after our last meal together. When her long lashes drifted down to veil her expression, I forced back the wild need to nudge her chin up, to see the evidence of the chemistry that heated the very air around us.

'Doesn't mean I have to eat with *you*,' she murmured.

For some absurd reason I bit back another smile, and the urge to keep tangling with her spiralled through me.

'I won't sully your meal with my presence, if that is your wish.'

Surprise jerked her gaze back to me. 'You won't?'

'I have a few more business matters to deal with. You can eat while I take care of them.'

The knock on the door at that moment drew her suspicion.

'You've already ordered lunch, haven't you?'

I shrugged. 'On the off-chance that you'd agree to stay, yes.'

'There's nothing "off-chance" about anything you do, but nice try,' she sniped.

As she headed to the sofa and I returned to my desk, my smile turned resolute. She had no idea how accurate her words were. How meticulously I intended to seal her completely into my life.

If this child was mine—and, *Christos*, I would burn the world down if I'd been fooled for a second time—then nothing in all existence would stop me from claiming it.

For two hours I attempted to ignore her disquieting presence, to concentrate on laying the groundwork for what needed to be done. But with every appreciative bite of the meal I'd had my chef prepare for her, with every stretch of her voluptuous body as she shifted on the sofa and every flick of her hair over her shoulder, my body reacted with visceral hunger.

A hunger I cursed with every breath for messing with my concentration and control. For being neither circumspect nor discerning about the kind of woman it wanted.

First Anneka, with her wide-eyed innocence that had hidden a grotesquely flawed character. Now this green-eyed siren, who should be the last woman to pique my interest and yet fired me up with one simple defiant look.

'You're glaring at me,' she stated, while glaring right back.

I ended a call that was going nowhere fast, rose and approached her. With each step I knew the path I was taking was the right one. Swift. Precise.

*Permanent?*

She would resist my plans, of course. I chose to ignore the kick in my gut signalling that I'd relish tussling with her. This was more than base pleasure. This was laying the foundations to secure my heir's future.

Her stunning green eyes widened a touch, and I was gratified to see her gaze rush over me before she attempted to look away.

'Did you enjoy your lunch?'

She shrugged. 'It was fine, thanks.'

Her gaze grew more wary the closer I got. Did she know how enthralling she looked, with her face tilted up to me like that, the satin-smooth perfection of her neck just begging to be stroked?

For several heartbeats after I stopped, she stared at me. Then she visibly roused herself, picked up her purse and rose.

'I should be going. If I'm lucky, I might catch an earlier flight.'

'You're aware we have a lot more to discuss?'

She paused. 'Like what?'

'Like your employment status, for starters. Have you secured another job since the incident at the clinic?'

Her gaze swept away. 'Not a permanent one. I'm currently temping.'

I forced my jaw not to grit. 'Are you going to tell me what you meant about your mother?'

Her chin lifted at that. 'No. It's still none of your business.'

'The welfare of this child is paramount. Nothing is going to stop me ensuring it doesn't come to harm. I wish you to be absolutely clear about that.'

'And you intend to dig your way through my life to do that?' she challenged.

'I intend to take away whatever worries you so that you can concentrate on remaining healthy.'

The answer disarmed her. As it had been intended to. Her lips parted, triggering a shot of heat to my groin.

'You…can't do that.'

'Can't I? How exactly do you propose to stop me?'

Her eyes sparkled with that telling green that spelled the start of her temper. 'A restraining order, for starters?'

I curbed the curious smile that threatened. 'What's to stop me from returning the favour? Or have you forgotten the small matter of your crime?'

Vexation receded, to be replaced by apprehension. 'I'm getting tired of your veiled threats, Mr Xenakis.'

'I said you may call me Neo.'

One elegant eyebrow quirked. 'Oh, I can use your first name now, can I?'

A touch of regret zinged through me. 'You'll have to excuse me for not being at my best that day. I wasn't aware that a tangible part of my future had been affected until I heard your news. It was hard to deal with. Almost as I hard as it was for you to deliver the news to me, perhaps?'

After a beat, she shook her head. 'It wasn't easy, no. I guess it's fair you'd want to put it behind you.'

Memories of the passionate way that day had ended blazed hot and insistent. 'Not all aspects of it. And, as it turns out, it will be impossible to do so now.'

Again awareness flashed in her luminous eyes, before she shrugged and took a few steps away from me.

'It is what it is. Now, I'd really like to make that flight, so if you don't mind…?'

I let her leave, granting us both a moment's necessary reprieve. But within seconds of her walking out, I was back at my desk. A quick phone call to my assistant with a handful of immediate action instructions, and I was heading out through the door.

She was already in the lift, her gaze triumphant as the steel doors slid shut between us. I called the next one, further unsettled by the whisper of a smile that I felt curve my lips. I frowned it off.

This was no smiling matter.

When Ax had delivered the news of his unexpected son I experienced a moment's searing jealousy, even while being overjoyed at his good fortune. But I also witnessed his despair at missing his son's first few months.

*Nothing* would come between me and every step of my child's growth in its mother's womb. Nor a single moment of its life.

*If it's yours.*

Seven months. For the chance at fatherhood I believed had been cruelly snatched away by a computer mistake, I would endure the torturous wait.

She rounded on me the moment I stepped out of the lift, the tail of her long hair a swinging, living flame I wanted to wrap around my fist.

'Really? You've instructed your goons to stop me from leaving?' she spat out.

'I have done nothing of the sort. Wendell is aware of my intention to give you a lift to the airport and he merely wished for you to wait for me. Isn't that so, Wendell?' I arched a brow at the stoic ex-military man.

'Precisely, sir.'

Sadie rolled her eyes. 'You two make a cracking comedy duo. Can I leave now?'

'Of course.'

She looked surprised when I held the door for her. How had the male she'd indulged in that brief relationship with treated her? Clearly not well enough, if a little chivalry surprised her. What about her mother?

Registering that I knew next to nothing about the woman

who was possibly carrying my child rankled. Enough to make me grow absent-minded as I slid my hand around her waist.

She started, her breath hitching as she shifted away from my touch and stepped dangerously close the kerb.

I caught her arm, stemming momentary panic. 'Easy, *pethi mou.*'

'I… You startled me, that's all.'

'I merely touched you to guide you to the car.'

Her translucent skin flushed again, the captivating sweep of her long lashes brushing her cheeks as she blinked. 'Well, I wasn't expecting it.'

The car drew up. I waved the driver away and opened the door for her. With another flick of her green eyes, she slid in. I followed, tightening my gut against the punch of lust that hit me at the display of one smooth, shapely leg.

The fact that she seemed determined to secrete herself as far away from me as possible when I joined her triggered a bolt of disgruntlement. Was I really that fearsome?

*Yes. You all but slapped on the handcuffs both times she attempted to contact you.*

Perhaps I *had* been fearsome—whereas Sadie, both times, had been…brave.

Registering the path of my thoughts, the new respect for her actions, I sheared off the notion. It remained to be seen whether her motives were truly altruistic.

And if they weren't?

The sheer depth of my hollow dread unnerved me. Enough for me to step away from it—leave it alone in a way I'd left nothing alone for as long as I could remember. I wasn't ready to tackle *what if*s. Especially the ever-growing one that demanded credentials as to my suitability as a father. Not yet.

What I *could* do was lay further bricks for the lockdown I had in mind.

'Xenakis Aeronautics is expanding into Latin America—

specifically Brazil and Argentina. But my marketing team are struggling to find traction for our newest marketing venture.'

Interest flickered in her gaze. 'What's the problem?' she asked after a handful of seconds.

'We beta-tested our new airline cabin six months ago, to rousing success, but the take-up fell sharply after three months.'

'What does this new cabin deliver? How is it different from other airline cabins?'

Did she realise she'd leaned forward? That her eyes sparkled with interest and intelligence? Clearly this was a subject she liked. Which begged the question of what had happened to stall her studies.

'They're like suites—one step up from first class, but not out of the realms of affordability for the successful individual.'

'I've seen promotional stuff from other airlines. If your cabins are two-person berths only…'

She paused as I shook my head. 'They range from two to six.'

Her eyes widened. 'That's…amazing. But I bet your team's marketing plan was to target billionaires and oligarchs who have more money than they know what do with?'

She'd hit the nail right on the head. 'Something like that.'

Her pert nose wrinkled in a grimace. 'Which begs the question—why would this oligarch fly in a superclass suite on a premium airline when he could charter his own plane? It'll most likely be for the bragging rights, which will lose their lustre after a handful of flights. I'm confident that's why you're experiencing a drop-off. You need to refine the suites. Since they can accommodate up to six, why not attract an entirely different demographic? Besides the luxury and exclusivity of having a suite to yourself on a commercial airline, the unique design also offers privacy.'

'What would be your plan if *you* were in charge?'

She grew even more animated, her eyes sparkling brighter. 'Oh, that's simple. I'd push hard to attract young, successful millennial families. Believe me, there's nothing worse than having an irate child kicking the back of your seat for hours on a long-haul flight. I can't imagine what it's like for harried parents having to apologise to disgruntled passengers. This will be a win-win for everyone. So why not market the suites to those who will welcome peace and quiet together with luxury and exclusivity? I'm assuming your suites are on the upper deck, like the others I've seen?'

I was a little put out that she knew more about my rivals' products than mine. 'Not only that, the Xen Suites come with premium sound insulation.'

She nodded enthusiastically. 'Just think how much that would appeal to the parents with young families who can afford it. And if you have a loyalty programme in place, where passengers can aspire to use of the suites, then it will boost the uptake even further.'

'The Xen Loyalty Programme is one of the best in the industry.'

'But I bet there's a steep points rise from, say, business class to superior class?'

I shrugged noncommittally.

She gave me a wry look. 'On the basis that I'm right, I'd offer incentives for the target demographic to try the suites for a limited period. I'm confident you'll see a sustained growth.'

'Are you, now?'

About to respond, most likely with a tart rejoinder to my droll tone, she glanced out of the window, then performed a double take.

'Why are we here?'

'You wished to return to England, did you not?' I replied.

'I assume that's your private jet?'

'You assume correctly. We have three hours, give or take,

before we land. A little longer after that to deliver you to your home. We can use that time for further discussions.'

Her enthralling green eyes widened. 'You…you're giving me a lift on your plane?'

'I wish to spare you and the baby the discomfort of a return journey in a cramped middle seat next to malodorous passengers.'

Colour tinged her cheeks, drawing my attention to their smoothness, reminding me of other sensational areas of her body. I shifted, willing the blood racing to my groin to slow.

'But—'

'My pilot is waiting on the steps. That means we have a fast-closing window for take-off. So perhaps we can continue your objections aboard?'

Her lips firmed. 'That sort of defeats the object of the exercise, doesn't it?'

'Are you really that attached to your budget airline seat?'

'Fine. You've made your point.'

*'Efkharisto.'*

'I don't know what that means.'

'It means *thank you.*'

'Oh. Okay.'

Despite having won this hand, I was reluctant to leave the car…to end the moments of accord we'd shared. Reinforcing my guard, I stepped out, telling myself it was only decent manners that made me hold out my hand to her.

She took it, stepped out and immediately released it.

The balmy early evening air drifted a breeze through the hangar, sliding her dress against her hips as she preceded me up the stairs. That hot tug of lust flamed in my groin, reminding me that the months before and after Sadie's eruption into my life had been the longest time I'd gone without a woman.

The notion that if my plan were to succeed I'd have to endure an even longer spell filled me with unwelcome dissatisfaction as I entered the plane after her.

Most people who were lucky enough to be invited onto the Xenakis jet frothed at the mouth at the no-expense-spared opulence of its interior.

One of four in the fleet of Jumbo Jets used for family and business trips, the Airbus was satisfyingly immense. With upper and lower decks, and filled with sleep, entertainment and business facilities, and even a twenty-seater cinema, it catered to every imaginable taste.

Anneka had loved to travel in this lap of luxury, insisting on the use of the jet several times a week during our engagement. Of course, I'd later found out what those trips had entailed…

Sadie's gaze flitted over hand-stitched cashmere throws, bespoke incorporated furniture and Aubusson carpeting with disarming lack of interest, her feet almost dragging as she contemplated the seats she could occupy, then made a beeline for a detached club chair.

About to follow, I paused when my phone buzzed in my pocket. Catching the attendant's eye, I nodded to Sadie. 'Get Miss Preston whatever she wants to eat and drink. Make sure she's comfortable.'

'Of course, sir.'

With more than a tinge of regret, I answered my phone. Then spent the next two hours putting the finishing touches on my plan to ensure an unbreakable alignment with Sadie Preston.

By the time we landed at the private airport twenty minutes from her North London residence, I was satisfied with my decisions. Enough to be confident that I could counter any argument she might have.

Once I'd dealt with the handful of obstacles still standing in my way.

The first came in the form of Martha Preston—a woman bearing a striking resemblance to her daughter, whose red hair Sadie had obviously inherited.

'You must be Mrs Preston,' I said when she appeared at the door. 'My name is—'

'My goodness—you're Neo Xenakis! Please, come in.' She threw the door wide open, much to her daughter's initial astonishment, then immediate annoyance.

'Mum—'

'Is something wrong?' Martha asked, hurrying down the hallway while throwing wide-eyed looks over her shoulder. 'When you said you'd be gone all day I assumed it was to work, not… Wow… Um… Anyway, welcome to our home, Mr Xenakis.'

'Thank you,' I said, unable to suppress my shudder as I looked around.

This squashed, dilapidated structure wasn't a home fit for anyone, never mind the woman who carried my child. I might not have the right emotional advantages to offer this child, but in this I could offer full benefits. My child would not be spending a second in this place. Nor would its mother.

'Can I get you anything? A drink? We have tea. Or coffee. Or—'

'He won't be staying long, Mum. He has things to do. Don't you?' Sadie enquired pointedly.

Martha Preston ignored her daughter, her smile at me widening. *Kalos*, the mother was going to be a breeze to handle.

I stepped into the even more cluttered living room of this house Sadie wouldn't be occupying for much longer, suppressing another smile even while calculating how quickly I could move.

Magazines of every description covered every available shabby surface, and a gaily coloured sofa was the only bright spot in the dank space. A look passed between mother and daughter before they both faced me.

'I'll take a rain check on that coffee, if I may, Mrs Preston. But I do have a request.'

Green eyes similar to her daughter's widened. 'Of course. Anything.'

Sadie frowned. Opened her mouth.

I beat her to it. Because, really, what was the point in dragging out the inevitable?

'I hope you'll forgive my bluntness, but I would be honoured if you'll give me your blessing to marry your daughter.'

Shock gripped me for a second before I rounded on this towering force of a man who'd gone from complete disavowal of his child to a systematic, head-spinning takeover in the last few hours.

'What? Are you out of your mind?'

'Sadie! Where are your manners? I'd like to think I brought you up better than this. I do beg your pardon, Mr Xenakis. And, please, call me Martha.'

My mother all but simpered at Neo, who inclined his head in gracious forgiveness for my bad manners.

I ground my teeth, partly to hold back my shock and partly with fury at his heartless joke. Because he had to be joking! Or, worse, this was payback for the prank he still believed I was playing on him.

'Please don't make excuses for me, Mum. And while you're at it, forget what Mr Xenakis just said. He didn't mean it.' I fired a telling glare at him, communicating my dim view of his actions.

His expression didn't change from one of intractable determination. For some reason, instead of angering me even more, that sent a sliver of a thrill through me. Until common sense prevailed.

'It's Neo, Sadie. You can't very well keep calling me Mr Xenakis when we're man and wife, can you?' he drawled.

'Since that's not going to happen, it's neither here nor there.'

The trace of the civility I was sure he'd cultivated for my

mother's benefit evaporated, allowing me an even clearer glimpse of the flint-hard resolution in his eyes. Cold foreboding gripped my nape, then slithered down my spine.

While I grappled with it, he turned to my mother with suave smoothness. 'This is a shock, I know. Besides, it's late. I don't wish to keep you up, Martha, but I would be pleased if you'd let me pick up our acquaintance again soon?'

I opened my mouth to counter his words.

The look in his eyes stopped me.

'Of course,' my mother replied, and then, for the first time in a long time, the hazy cloak she clung to, so she wouldn't have to face harsh reality, lifted. Her eyes glinted with steel as she stared at Neo. 'As to your admittedly surprising question—I'll speak to my daughter first. Clearly you two need better communication. When I'm satisfied that this is what she wants, you can have my blessing.'

Her answer didn't cow Neo. If anything, reinvigorated tenacity vibrated from him, filling up every spare inch of the living room.

Inclining his head in an almost regal way, he smiled. 'Very well. May I have a private word with your daughter?'

With a few words and what I expected was a hint of blushing, my mother left the room.

Unable to stand so close to him without losing my mind, or dissolving into hysterics, I hurried across the room, before whirling around. 'I don't know what the hell you think you're playing at, but—'

'I warned you I intended to do whatever it takes when it comes to this baby, did I not?' he said, in the even tone he'd used that day in his office two months ago. The one that announced he was chillingly rational. That every word from his lips had been calculated and calibrated to achieve the result he wanted.

A shiver raced down my body, urging me to stay in the present. To give every scrap of attention to this insane moment, lest I was swept away. 'This is… What are you doing?' I finally managed, when my head stopped spinning.

'Taking steps to secure my legacy.'

'Your *legacy*? You don't even fully accept that this baby is yours!'

He shrugged off the accusation. 'I've given it some thought and I've concluded that for the moment we'll proceed as if the child is mine.'

'Oh, wow. Lucky me.'

My sarcasm bounced off him. 'You got on a plane and travelled two and a half thousand miles to convince me. This is me meeting you halfway.'

'No, this is you bulldozing your way into my life with zero regard for what I want.'

He paused, folded his arms across his wide chest. 'Indulge me, then. Tell me some of what those wants are.'

I opened my mouth to tell him the paramount one. That I wanted him to leave. But with this new level of ruthless determination wouldn't I simply be postponing the inevitable?

'Permit me to start. Do you want a stable home for our child?'

'Of course I do.'

He nodded in that arrogant way that stated he'd scored a point for himself.

'What else, Sadie?' he urged softly. Oh, so dangerously.

I shrugged. 'I want what every normal person wants. To keep a roof over my head and to stop worrying about how to make ends meet.'

He looked around the living room, his face carefully neutral. 'I have several roofs. You will be welcome to any you choose.'

My mouth dropped open, but he was still talking. 'Were you serious about finishing your degree?'

'Of course.'

'There will be nothing standing in your way, should you choose to see things my way. As for your mother—'

'She's still none of your business.'

'Very well. When the time comes, and you confirm my suspicions, that too will be dealt with.'

Everything I wanted. Offered on a platter. Just like that. I gasped as the penny dropped. 'My God, this is why you stalled me in your office all afternoon and offered to give me a ride home? So you could chess move your way into my life?'

He didn't bother to deny it. 'I merely took time to ensure my plan was sound.'

'I'm not a damned charity case!'

'No,' he replied with heart-stopping brevity, as something close to awe flashed across his face. 'But according to every imaginable statistic, what is happening is a miracle. The baby you're carrying is a miracle.' Then that staggering determination returned. 'One I don't intend to let slip through my fingers.'

I wasn't sure whether to be angry or horrified at his calculated move.

'Don't overthink it, Sadie. I've simply come up with a plan to remove any stumbling blocks that will prevent what we both want from happening. You have needs. I can satisfy them. It's as simple as that,' he drawled arrogantly.

If he'd discovered a handwritten wish list crafted by me he wouldn't have been off by even a fraction. But what he was suggesting was unthinkable.

*Marriage?* I shook my head. 'Even if everything you've listed is true, and I want all of it, why would I bind myself to you?'

'Because I can give you everything you want. All you have to do is marry me.'

I laughed then, because all this insanity needed an outlet. Before I spontaneously combusted. When his eyes narrowed ominously, I laughed harder.

'Is this just a trait of all insanely wealthy men, or are

you cursed with the notion that you can throw your weight around like this and get what you want?'

He didn't answer immediately. Instead he sauntered towards me, his gaze locked on my face as he approached.

'You feel the need to resist and rail at what you see as my overbearing move when this is merely accelerating a necessary and efficient process.'

Laughter dried up in my throat. 'But why marriage?'

'No Xenakis child has been born out of wedlock. I don't intend for my child to be the first.'

'Here's an idea. Buck the trend. This is the twenty-first century. Set your own path.'

'No. I will not. Label me a traditionalist if you will, but in this I will not be swayed,' he replied with deep gravity.

'You forget that for you to achieve that you'll need my agreement.'

'And you will give it. I'm sure of it.'

'Are you? How? Let me guess—this is where you threaten me with criminal charges again unless I bend to your will?'

For the longest moment he remained silent, considering it. Then, astonishingly, he shook his head. 'That incident is in the past. It's time to turn the page. That transgression will no longer be held against you. Regardless of where we go from here, we will not speak of it again.'

Shocked relief burst through me. I searched his face for signs that he meant it and saw nothing but solid honesty.

*Where we go from here...*

Ominous words that rattled me as he stared at me. As with every second, the urge to consider his offer gathered strength.

To buy myself time, I countered, 'If you're standing there waiting for me to give you an answer, you're going to be disappointed.'

Something crossed his face that looked a little like alarm, but it was gone much too soon for me to decipher it.

'While you wrestle with that *yes* you're too stubborn to say, let's discuss other issues. I believe one has already been tackled?'

The head-spinning encroached. Again, removing myself from his immediate orbit, from the intoxicating scent of aftershave and warm skin that made me want to wrap my arms around his trim waist and bury my face in his neck, I crossed to the small pink-striped sofa we'd managed to rescue from the bailiff's clutches and sank into it.

'I wouldn't hold your breath,' I countered.

An arrogant smile twisted his lips. 'I'd like you to put the marketing plan you outlined into a report for me.'

Excitement of a different kind joined the chaos surging through me. 'Why?' I asked, forcing myself not to think of our conversation in the car on the way to the airport. Of my thrill when I solved his marketing problem. The grudging respect in his eyes as he sounded out my solutions. If he wanted a report, did that mean…?

'Because that will form the basis of your employment with Xenakis Aeronautics,' he said.

I was glad I was sitting down, because I was sure the shock would've floored me otherwise. 'What?'

'Your new role. As my intern starting as soon as we have an agreement.'

More puzzle pieces fell into place. 'All those questions in the car on the way to the airport…you were *interviewing* me?'

He nodded.

'And…?'

'And you presented a sound strategy—one worth consideration. The second you sign an employment contract I'll pass it on to my marketing team—of which you'll be a part. If you wish.'

I did wish. With every atom in my body, I wanted to grasp his offer with both hands.

But all this came at a price.

Neo Xenakis, marketing guru extraordinaire, wasn't handing round internships of a lifetime out of the goodness of his heart. He was bartering my wish list for complete access to my child.

But, even knowing that, I couldn't help pride and satisfaction fizzing through me like the headiest champagne. Regardless of what had led us here, to have the president of marketing for a global powerhouse like Xenakis Aeronautics pronouncing my idea sound was an accolade worth celebrating.

'Thanks, that's…um…a generous offer.'

'You're welcome,' he returned, and then for some inexplicable reason his gaze dropped to my mouth.

A moment later, I realised I was smiling. And he seemed…*fascinated*.

# CHAPTER SIX

THE MOMENT STRETCHED as we stared at one another, a tight little sensual bubble wrapping itself around us, making it hard to breathe as heat and need and desire filled my body.

This time he was the one who broke contact, his chest expanding on a long breath before he said, 'Which item do you wish to discuss next?'

*None*, I wanted to say. But, reluctantly buoyed by the promise of utilising my marketing knowledge, I wanted to hear him out. See where he was going with this.

'What do you suspect about my mother?'

He shrugged. 'That she's far too dependent on you— perhaps uses you as an emotional crutch to hide a deeper problem?'

I pressed my lips together, unwilling to betray my mother.

'Whatever those problems are, they'll only grow if ignored,' he said.

With a grimace, I exhaled. 'She gambles online. It's small sums, but—'

'Addiction like that is insidious, Sadie. It needs to be curbed now or it'll become a problem.'

Unable to meet his gaze, I toyed with the hem of my dress.

'Has it already become a problem?' he intuited smoothly.

The answer spilled out before I could stop it. 'Yes. I've spoken to her about it. Asked her to get help.'

His face hardened. 'You might have to be a little more insistent. Ruthless, even.'

'Like you?'

A look flashed in his eyes, but he shrugged. 'If it makes you feel better to think that way, then so be it.'

Temptation swelled higher. I knew I had to tackle my

mother's problem before I lost the only parent I had, but…
'She's my concern. I'll find her the help she needs.'

Neo nodded after a handful of seconds.

I licked my lips, knowing the most important topic still needed to be tackled. 'Let's talk about the baby.'

'Yes,' he replied, his voice deep and heavy, with that yearning that still had the power to rock me.

'How would it even work?'

'Our marriage would simply legitimise my child and for-malise any agreement as to childcare when it's dissolved.'

A beginning and an end. So…a temporary marriage. A get-out clause and a possible end to his duties as a father when the appeal wore off?

The sting of abandonment registered, deep and true, those flippant words in my father's letter burning through my brain.

'You're pulling out the stops to get what you want *now*. How do I know you'll even want to be a father when this baby is a reality? That you won't simply abandon him or her?'

The hands he'd shoved in his pockets slowly emerged. Purpose vibrated from him. But there was something else. A fleeting look of *doubt* which evaporated in the next in-stant as his confidence returned, expanding into the room as he strode forward and sank down in front of me.

This close, the look in his eyes captivated me, made me hold my breath.

'I've experienced what it feels like to believe that father-hood will never happen for me. The feeling is…indescrib-able. So perhaps this is one of the things you'll have to take on faith. I *want* this child, Sadie.'

The fervour brimming in his voice…

The implacable stare.

That…yearning.

I believed him. But…

'How long did you see this marriage deal continuing?'

He shrugged. 'For the sake of the child's stability and welfare, its first few years at the very least.'

'Then what?'

'Then we agree to whatever custody plan works in the best interests of our child.'

The response should have satisfied me, but something cold and tight knotted inside me. Neo might be in full negotiation mode, but at least he was laying all his cards on the table.

Unlike my father, who'd stuck around until the going got tough and then bailed, with a cruel little letter addressed to the daughter he'd claimed to love and cherish. His wife hadn't even received that courtesy—only a letter from his lawyer, inviting her to sue for divorce on the grounds of abandonment. It was an option my mother was yet to take, the shock and anguish of the abrupt turn her life had taken still keeping her in a fog of despair all these years later.

Wasn't it better this way? To know what was coming and prepare for it rather than be blindsided by it? Especially when until this morning the possibility that my child was going to start life knowing only one parent had been great? Could I pass up this opportunity on behalf of my child?

Neo leaned forward, bringing his power and his glory and that intoxicating scent into play. With one hand braced next to my thigh, he pinned me in place with his gaze for an interminable moment before he lifted the other hand to rest against my face.

Heat from his palm accelerated my pulse. My unguarded gasp echoed quietly between us, my heart wildly thundering as he slowly glided his thumb over my chin, my lower lip.

My insides were debating whether to flip over or melt when he said, 'It's better that we approach this with civility instead of conflict, Sadie.'

Deep, even-toned words that nevertheless gave me a glimpse of what it would be like to keep fighting him.

Jerking away before I did something stupid, like wrap

my lips around that masculine thumb, I shook my head. 'I need time. To think about this.'

Mutiny briefly glinted in his eyes before he gave an abrupt nod and surged to his full height. After a short pace round the living room, he faced me again.

'I have a family function to attend in Athens tomorrow. A new nephew to meet,' he said, with a hint of something peculiar in his voice.

I couldn't tell whether it was anticipation, yearning or bitterness. Perhaps a combination of the three.

'How old is he?'

'I'm told he's almost four months old.'

Curiosity ate at me. 'How come you've never met him before?'

His jaw clenched for a taut stretch. 'Because no one in my family, including my brother, knew of his existence before a few weeks ago.'

So Axios had been in the dark about his son's existence? 'Why?'

He shrugged. 'The reasons for that will become clear tomorrow, I expect.' His gaze sharpened. 'You have until my return to consider my proposal.'

His words flung me back to the present. 'There was no proposal, as I recall. Only edicts thrown down and expected to be followed.'

'I merely set out the course of action I believe is best. If you have a better proposal I'm willing to hear you out.'

He said that while cloaked in an arrogant self-assurance that nothing I could come up with would beat his. Blatant certainty blazed in the gaze that held mine for a nerve-shredding minute.

Other sensations started to encroach. Ones that had heated me up from the inside when he'd touched my lips just now and made every stretch of skin his gaze lingered on burn with fierce awareness. It was as if he'd reached out and touched me again. Stroked me. Tasted me.

Intensely aware of my breath shortening, of the place between my legs growing damp and needy, I cleared my throat and stood. 'If we're done here…?'

He retraced his steps towards me, moving with lithe, attention-absorbing grace, his darkened eyes scouring my face one more time. From his pocket, he produced a graphite-grey business card, embossed with the iconic dark gold picture of the phoenix etched into every Xenakis plane's tail fin. The card simply read *N. Xenakis* and listed a mobile number.

'My personal cell. Use it whenever you wish.'

His fingers brushed mine as I took it. At my shallow inhalation, his eyes darkened.

It struck me then that there was one subject we hadn't discussed.

Neo was a virile, magnificent specimen of a man. One who wouldn't be short of female companionship, should he wish it. Did he intend this proposed marriage to come with the certain leeway rumoured to happen within marriages of conveniences like this?

Even while my mind screamed that it would be the rational course to take, my chest tightened, everything inside me rebelling at the idea.

*So what would your solution be?*

I ignored the snide little voice attempting to prod me into admitting the secret yearning that had no place in this transaction. What happened two months ago had been an aberration. One that had produced consequences we needed to prioritise now. There could be no repeat of it.

So why were my feet leaden as I followed him to the door? Why did my gaze avidly catalogue his every feature as he stepped out, turned and murmured, 'I'll be in touch'?

And why, when I tossed and turned and sleep wouldn't come, when I should have been thinking about what was best for my child, my mother, my career, did I keep returning to that ever-growing knot of anxiety over whether Neo would take a lover outside of our marriage…or if there already *was* one?

'Is there something I should know, Sadie?'

I'd expected the question. Frankly, I was surprised my mother had waited till morning to ask. Now she stared at me over her teacup, worry reflected in her eyes.

I took a deep breath. 'I'm pregnant, Mum. I'm sorry I didn't tell you before, but—'

'You wanted to tell the father first?' she inserted gently, with no judgement and no surprise over the news. 'I'm assuming Neo Xenakis is the father?'

'Yes. I told him yesterday.'

Another sip of tea, then with a short nod she accepted my news. 'And that's why he wants to marry you?' she asked, visibly holding her breath.

'Yes.'

A smile bloomed across her face. 'Oh, Sadie, that's so romantic.' Her eyes sparkled, much as they had last night, when she'd opened the door to Neo.

'Please, Mum, don't get carried away. This isn't like one of your magazine love stories.'

'Oh, *pffi*. A man like that wouldn't offer marriage unless he was hell-bent on permanence. But is it what *you* want?'

Weariness dragged at me. 'I don't know.'

Her sparkle dimmed. Nevertheless, she reached across the small kitchen table and laid her hand over mine. 'Whatever you decide, I'll support you, sweetheart.'

My eyes prickled, my heart turning over with the knowledge that I loved my mother too much to remain blind to the dangerous road she was treading with her gambling.

About to broach the subject, I froze when the doorbell rang. With a curiously trepidatious expectancy, I answered the door.

A courier held a large, expensive-looking box in his

hand. 'Delivery for Sadie Preston from Xenakis?' the young man asked, eyebrows raised.

Senses jumping, I signed for it.

In the living room, I set it on the coffee table, a reluctance to open it rippling through me. Because, more than not wanting whatever lay within the square box, I was terrified I would *like* whatever Neo had sent me. An expensive something, judging by the discreet logo signifying the endorsement of English royalty often attached to exclusive items.

When the suspense got too much, I tore it open.

The box was filled to the brim with packets of handmade biscuits, each exquisitely wrapped with a thin silver bow. On top of the first one lay a small white envelope, with a note within that read:

*I'm told these help with morning sickness. Be so kind as to try not to forget to eat them.*

Rolling my eyes seemed like the perfect counterfoil for the smile that insistently tugged at my lips. The man was insufferable.

*And he thinks the baby you claim is his might not be.*

My smile evaporated, my heart growing heavy as I plucked out one neatly wrapped packet and opened it. The scent of ginger was oddly pleasant, and not vomit-inducing like most smells these days. Apprehensively, I bit into the biscuit, stemming a moan at the heavenly taste. Experiencing no ill effects, I finished one small pack, and reached for another.

'I see your Greek god means business. I bet he had these flown in on one of his private jets?'

I jumped and turned to see my mum in the doorway, beaming as her eyes lit on the box.

'You know what he does for a living?'

'Of course I know! You'd have to be living under a rock

not to know about the Xenakis dynasty. Rumour is they've surpassed the Onassis family in wealth and stature. Shame what happened to your fella, though.'

I frowned. 'He's not "my fella"—and what are you talking about?'

Like a magician's big reveal, she produced a tabloid magazine from behind her back. 'I went digging the moment I left the living room last night. Aren't you glad I keep all my magazines, instead of chucking them in the bin like you keep pushing me to?'

I didn't answer, because my gaze was locked on the crimson headline.

*Neo Xenakis Emerges from Three-Week Coma... Ends Year-Long Engagement.*

Ignoring the fine tremor in my hands, I scoured the article, concluding very quickly that while the reporter had one or two facts, the majority of the piece was conjecture. But the bit that read, *By mutual consent, Neo Xenakis and Anneka Vandenberg, the Dutch supermodel, have agreed to go their separate ways* clearly had some truth to it.

The reality that I had very little knowledge about the man I was marrying attacked me again in that moment.

Then the very thought that I was leaning towards acceptance of this temporary arrangement slammed into me hard, making my heart lurch.

I told myself I was remedying the former when I retreated to the bedroom and dialled his number the moment my mother flicked on the TV and grew absorbed in the soap she was watching.

He answered immediately. 'Sadie.'

The deep, sexy growl of my name sent sensation flaring through my body.

Tightening my grip on the phone, as if it would stop the

flow of pure need, I launched straight into it. 'You were engaged before?'

He inhaled sharply, then I heard the sound of footsteps as the background conversation and music faded.

His heavy silence brimmed with displeasure. 'There are aspects of my past that have no bearing on what's happening between you and I,' he said eventually.

Unreasonable hurt lanced me. 'According to *you*. You felt entirely comfortable digging into *my* life. I think quid pro quo earns me the same rights,' I said, despite the sensation that I was treading on dangerous personal ground.

'I furnished myself with details of your past only as far as it pertained to the welfare of my child. But if you must know, yes, the tabloids back then got that piece of information right.'

'What else did they get right? What else do I need to know about you?'

*Did you love her? Why did it end?*

'You want more personal details, Sadie? Then marry me.'

My breath caught, those two words tapping into a secret well I didn't want to acknowledge. Because within that well dwelt a fierce yearning to belong. But to be worthy of consideration for *myself*, not like in the past, because it suited my father's professional ladder climbing, or because I was carrying Neo's child now.

'Will you marry me, Sadie?' he pressed, his voice low and deep.

'It's nice to be asked. Finally. And thanks for answering my question.'

'No—*efkharisto*,' he breathed heavily.

Yesterday he'd said that meant *thank you*. Surprise held me mute for a second. 'For what?'

'For going the extra mile to tell me about the pregnancy even when I made things…unpleasant.'

'You're welcome. But still…why?'

'Because, as much as my brother is overjoyed at the existence of his son, the time he's missed weighs on him. I wouldn't have wished that for myself.'

'Oh.' I drew in a shaky breath as that unique place inside me threatened to soften.

Silence echoed down the line. When he ended it, his voice was tense. 'Do you have an answer for me, Sadie?'

My heart lurched, then thundered as if I was on the last leg of a marathon. 'That depends...'

'On?' he bit out.

'On whether your status two months ago still holds true. I know this marriage will be in name only, but if I'm going to make someone "the other woman", even for a short while, I'd like to be forewarned.'

The background noise had faded completely, leaving the steady sound of his breathing to consume every inch of my attention.

'You have my word that there is no other woman, and nor will there be as long as this agreement between us stands.'

Even as the knot inside me inexplicably eased, that last addition sent a bolt of disquiet through me. I smashed it down, dwelling on the positives in all of this. My child would be getting the best possible start in life. My mother would receive the help she'd denied she needed. I could concentrate on finishing my degree and finally starting the career I'd yearned for.

But, best of all, the fervour with which Neo wanted his child meant there wouldn't be a repeat of what my father had done to me. No postcard would ever land on my baby's doorstep, with a few words telling him or her that they'd been abandoned in favour of a better life.

So what if every facet of this agreement made me feel surplus to requirements? That, although my child wouldn't suffer the same fate, it felt as if I was reliving the past, and again others' needs had been placed above my own?

I couldn't deny that the benefits outweighed the momentary heartache. I would get over this. As long as I placed some firm rules of my own.

'There will be no sex in this marriage. Do you agree to that?'

A sharp intake of breath. 'What?' he demanded tightly.

'No sex. Or no deal.'

He uttered something long and terse in Greek. Time stretched, tight and tense. Then he growled, 'If that's your wish.'

I squeezed my eyes shut, hoping for a miracle solution that didn't involve committing myself to a far too magnetically captivating man for the foreseeable future.

*You've already been given a miracle.*

Whatever had happened to make him believe he couldn't father children, our encounter had proved otherwise. We simply needed to make the best of the situation.

'Sadie?' His voice throbbed with authority that said he wouldn't be denied.

With a deep breath, I gave my answer. 'Yes. I'll marry you.'

He exhaled, then said briskly, 'Good. I will be in touch shortly.'

I blinked in surprise at the abrupt end to the call. But what had I expected? Trumpets and confetti?

*He's marrying you to secure his child. Get used to that reality.*

'Oh, Sadie.' My mother stood in the doorway, unapologetic about eavesdropping or the emotional tears spilling down her cheeks. 'I'm so thrilled for you, darling. You're doing the right thing.'

I wanted to tell her not to get her hopes up. But the words stuck in my throat, as the enormity of what I'd committed to flooded every corner of my being. When she swamped me in a tight hug, I let her effervescence counteract the quiet dismay flaring to life that reeked of what-the-hell-have-I-done?

'He won't let you down. Not like your father did. I'm confident of it.'

Financially? Perhaps not. Emotionally…?

I skittered away from that thought, wondering when my emotional well-being had become a factor. The idea of Neo and me was so out of the realms of possibility it was laughable.

So why didn't I feel like laughing? Why did the solid ground I should be stepping onto suddenly feel like quicksand?

That thought lingered, unanswered, throughout the dizzying set of events that followed.

Neo's almost offhand offer to me of his Mayfair property—*If you want to be more comfortable during the process*—had felt like another silken trap, but with homelessness a grim reality it was a lifeline I hadn't been able to refuse.

The property was a world away from the flat I'd left behind. The four-storey mansion sat on an exclusive street in an exclusive part of Mayfair, complete with a basement swimming pool and a stretch limo. A Rolls Royce Phantom and two supercars gleamed beneath recessed lights in the underground car park.

Within the house itself, every surface held breathtaking works of art and the kind of thoughtful blending of antique and contemporary decor that the wealthy either paid for through the teeth or put together with indulgent passion. Since Neo didn't seem the decorating type, I could only assume a king's ransom had been lavished on this place.

In the five immaculate suites, every last item of luxury had been provided—right down to the whirlpool baths and voice-controlled shower. An executive chef whose specialities included catering to expectant mothers presented herself within an hour of our arrival, then proceeded to whip up samples of exquisite meals for me to try.

And barely twenty-four hours after Neo's superefficient moving team had installed us in his property, the wedding spectacle commenced.

As did my arguments with Neo.

He'd soon found out that *leave it with me* when it came to the wedding wouldn't fly with me.

Three stages of wedding coordinator interviews were cut down to one, a dozen bids from the world-famous couture houses vying for the privilege of creating my wedding dress and trousseau, together with the present and upcoming seasons' day and evening wear, were whittled down from five designers to two.

The moment I'd managed to pick my jaw off the floor when I saw the wedding guest list, and stopped my mother from swooning with delight at the ultra-five-star treatment, I dialled Neo's number.

A heated twenty minutes later, we'd reached a compromise.

The wedding would be small, and the choice of dress mine alone. In turn, he would pick the venue—his private island in Greece—and the date—as soon as possible.

The only thing I didn't quibble over, was even grateful for, was the psychologist who arrived on the doorstep—despite knowing that this was simply another box being ticked by Neo on the journey to getting what he wanted.

The gambling conversation with my mother had been hard and tearful, and her acknowledgement that she had a problem and was still having a hard time dealing with my father's desertion had cracked my heart in two.

'I guess I should look forward now,' she'd said. 'You need me. I have a role as the mother of the bride and then as a grandmother.'

But within minutes of wiping her tears she had reached for her phone and excused herself, and minutes later, when

I'd approached her bedroom, I'd heard the distinct sound of electronic chips tumbling on a gaming site.

Heart heavy, I had retreated.

Neo called out of the blue an hour later. Still a little out of sorts, I answered my phone.

He immediately grew tense. 'Is something the matter?'

I barely managed to stop a weary laugh from escaping. 'The better question is "what isn't?"'

Tight silence greeted me. 'You are not having second thoughts.'

It wasn't a question but more of an edict.

'Am I not?' I taunted, my nerves a little too frayed to play nice. 'I can't promise I won't send the next person who asks me how many undernotes I like scenting my vintage champagne packing.'

'That's all that's worrying you? Or is there something else? The prenup I sent over for your signature, maybe?'

The question was a little too tight, like a dangerously coiled spring, set to explode.

My gaze slid to a copy of the prenuptial agreement a sharply dressed lawyer had hand delivered a few hours before. I frowned at the curious note in Neo's voice.

'What about it? It's already signed, if that's what you're calling about.'

A stunned silence greeted my response. 'You *signed* it?'

'Yes. Why are you surprised?'

'I'm not,' he drawled. And before I could call him out, he rasped, 'Tell me what's wrong.'

I let the subject of his peculiar attitude over the prenup go as I toyed with sharing my worries about my mother with him. The reminder that the baby I was carrying was the only thing Neo was interested in stopped me.

'I'm not changing my mind, if that's what you're worried about.'

He exhaled audibly, making me realise he'd been holding his breath. Had he been prepared to launch another vanquishing skirmish should I have responded differently?

'That's a wise course of action.'

For some reason that response hurt. I smothered the sting. 'Was there something in particular you wanted?'

'Yes. To give you the date for our wedding. It'll happen two weeks from tomorrow. That gives you a week to finalise your affairs before you come to Greece.'

Since the internship was at the head office in Athens, I'd agreed to the move.

'My mother's coming with me. A change of scene will help with her outlook on life.'

'I'm not a monster, Sadie. Regardless of where she chooses to stay, she'll receive the counselling she needs. But you must accept that our agreement includes not over-burdening yourself with tasks that are out of your control. I will not allow it.'

I knew he was dishing out the hard truth, and I wanted to hate Neo. But deep down I knew that had circumstances been different, had I been granted other choices, I still would have chosen this. An internship at Xenakis. A chance to live in a different country, experience another culture. All of it.

Except staying within the orbit of this man who turned my equilibrium inside out?

Maybe…

The objections I wanted to hurl at him died in my throat, and exactly two Saturdays later my breath caught, as it had been catching seemingly every other second, as the ten-seater luxury helicopter my mother and I were ensconced in circled over a large island in the middle of the Aegean in preparation to land.

The island was mostly flat, bursting with green and pink foliage and large stretches of stunning white beaches. But on the northernmost point a bluff rose sharply over the water, where towering waves crashed against menacing-looking rocks below.

Magnificent, mesmerising, awe-inspiring—but also dangerous in places.

Just like its owner.

Several small houses, most likely staff accommodation, dotted the right side of the island, after which came extensive stables, a large paddock with thoroughbreds being tended to by stable hands.

The aircraft banked, granting a first view of the resplendent villa and grounds in the mid-afternoon sun.

'Oh, my God,' my mother whispered.

The sentiment echoed inside me.

Spread beneath us was the most magnificent sight I'd ever seen. The sprawling whitewashed villa was divided into two giant wings the size of football fields and connected by an immense glass-roofed living area that could easily accommodate a thousand guests. A sparkling swimming pool abutted the living area, and a tiered lawn went on almost for ever, ending at a large gazebo set right on the beach, complete with twin hammocks set to watch the perfect sunset.

I was still drenched in awe when the scene of the wedding ceremony came into view.

Unlike the spectacle of his brother's wedding—the details of which my mother had delighted in showing me via her magazines—Neo had agreed to a close-family-only wedding. The handful of guests were perched on white-flower-decorated seats, laid out on a blinding white carpet on the vast landscaped lawn. The 'altar' was bursting with white and pink Matthiola, specially imported from Italy, and the florists' gushing use of the flower meant to symbolise lasting beauty and a happy life echoed in my mind as the chopper landed.

The walk from the aircraft to where Neo's family members had risen to their feet felt like a trek across a field of landmines, my pulse leaping with apprehension with each step, the sea-tinged breeze lifting my organza and lace wedding dress, reminding me how far away I was from normal reality.

I was marrying a wealthy, powerful man. One who'd proved he could bend the path of destiny itself to his will. One who was assuming greater and greater occupation in my thoughts.

One who bristled with impatience as my steps faltered.

Beside Neo, a man matching his height murmured to him, a kind of hard amusement twitching his lips. Neo sent him a baleful glare before his eyes locked on mine, compelling me with the sheer force of his dynamism.

Despite our many charged conversations, I hadn't seen him since the night of his skewed proposal. His designer stubble was gone, and the lightning-strike effect of his clean-shaven face stalled my feet completely.

Somewhere along this journey I'd fooled myself into thinking I could handle an association with this powerful man. Now, I wasn't so sure. How could I be when his very presence struck me with such alarming emotions?

The man next to him stepped forward, momentarily distracting me.

Axios Xenakis—Neo's older brother.

He approached, eyeing me with the same piercing Xenakis gaze, unashamedly assessing me before the barest hint of a smile lifted the corners of his mouth.

He placed himself next to me and, with a nod at my mother, offered me his arm. 'As much as I'm enjoying seeing my brother twisting in the wind, perhaps you'd be so kind as to have a little mercy?'

'I'm not doing anything…' I murmured.

'Precisely. You are merely hesitating long enough for him to feel the kick of uncertainty. Believe me, I know what *that* feels like.'

His words were directed at me but his gaze flicked to a dark-haired, stunningly beautiful woman cradling an adorable baby in her arms. They shared a heated, almost inde-

cently sensual look that would have made me cringe had my
whole attention not been absorbed by the man I'd pledged
to marry. The man who looked a whisker away from issu-
ing one of those terse little commands that irritated and
burned but also flipped something in my stomach while
getting him what he wanted.

What he wanted, clearly, was for me to honour my word.

One hand twitched, and it was as if a layer of that supreme control slipped as he watched me.

*Think of Mum. Think of the baby.*

Knowing he was eager to secure his child delivered a
numb kind of acceptance over me. Helped propel me to
where he stood.

He exhaled, and just like that control was restored.

The ceremony went off without a hitch. Probably because
Neo had forbidden any.

In what seemed like a breathless, head-spinning minute
I was married to one of the most formidable men on earth.
And he was turning to me, his fierce gaze locked on my lips.

It was all the warning I got before he leaned down, his
lips warm and dangerously seductive as they brushed mine
once. Twice. Then moved deeper for a bare second before
he raised his head.

His gaze blatantly raked me from head to toe, his nostrils flaring as his gaze lingered on my belly.

*'Dikos mou,'* he murmured beneath his breath.

'What?'

He started, as if realising he'd spoken aloud, then immediately collected himself. When he circled my wrist with
one hand and turned me to face the dozen or so guests, I
steeled myself against the fresh cascade of awareness dancing over my body—told myself it meant nothing, was simply
a continuation of whatever role he was playing. And when
he turned to rake his gaze from the swept-back, loosely
bound design the stylist had put my hair into, over my face

and down my body, before deeply murmuring, 'You look beautiful...' I told myself it was for the benefit of his family.

Barely minutes later, once the wait staff had begun circulating with platters of exquisite canapés and glasses of vintage champagne, Neo had grown aloof. A fine tension vibrated off him, increasing every time I tried to extricate myself from his hold.

When it grew too much I faced him, thankful that we were temporarily alone. 'Is something wrong?'

His expression grew even more remote. 'Should there be?'

I shrugged. 'You're the one who seems agitated.'

For a tight stretch of time, he didn't speak. Then, with piercing focus, he said, 'I commend you for holding up your end of the bargain, Sadie.'

Despite the backhanded compliment, his expression suggested he was waiting for the other shoe to fall.

I raised an eyebrow, eager to find a level footing with him, despite the cascade of emotions churning through me. Barely a month ago I'd been blissfully unaware that I carried a child. Now, I wasn't simply a mother-to-be, I was the wife of a formidable man from an equally formidable family.

'Does that win me some sort of brownie point?' I asked, more to cover the quaking intensifying within me than anything else—because, despite his expression, the fingers holding me prisoner were moving over my wrist, exploding tiny fireworks beneath my skin.

That touch of hardness tinged his smile. 'Sadly not. You had your chance to win more during the prenuptial agreement signing.' His gaze probed as if he were trying to unearth something. 'Perhaps you regret signing it now?'

I frowned. 'Why would I? There was nothing in there unacceptable to me. It seemed skewed in your favour—just as you wanted it, I suspect?'

He shrugged. 'As with any of my contracts, it seeks to

protect what's mine. But you've signed on that dotted line, so there's no going back.'

'I don't get what's going on here. You *wanted* me to throw a fit over the prenup?' I asked, puzzled. 'Why on earth would I do that?'

He tensed, a flash of disconcertion darkening his eyes before he erased it. 'That was one scenario. But, seeing as you signed it, let's not dwell on it. The deed is done.' His gaze dropped to my belly again. 'Now we wait,' he breathed.

# CHAPTER SEVEN

His words seeped deep into my bones, robbed me of breath.

For one tiny minute I'd forgotten that Neo harboured a very large question mark over my baby's paternity. That every term he'd negotiated and every luxury he'd tossed at my feet in his relentless pursuit of possessing the child I carried had come with the unspoken clause that he was hedging his bets. That my word wasn't good enough.

And where I'd have shrugged off the accusation a month ago, these past two weeks had weakened my foundations, wilting me enough that the barbs burrowed through the cracks. And stuck.

Worse, I only had myself to blame—because his endgame, like my father's, hadn't changed.

This time when I tugged my hand away he released me, although his lips tightened for a nanosecond. 'What's the matter?'

Our progression over the lush green grass had brought us to a section of the never-ending garden with luxurious bespoke seats set around beautifully decorated low tables, more in the style of an elegant garden party than a wedding reception.

He stopped at the seats that were set up on a dais and, beckoning one of the sharply dressed waiters carrying platters of food, helped himself to two gold-rimmed plates overflowing with Greek delicacies.

'Why, absolutely nothing,' I answered, plastering on a bright, patently fake smile.

He started to frown. I looked away, only to catch Ax's watchful gaze.

I turned back to Neo. 'Does your brother know why you...why we...?'

'We're married, Sadie. I'm your husband. You're my wife. You'll have to get used to saying it. Try the chicken,' he said, holding out a silver-skewered morsel to me.

The scent of lemon and rosemary wafted towards me enticingly, but I hesitated, refusing to let that bewildered fizzing inside me gain traction. 'You didn't answer my question.'

He dropped the food back onto the plate, his jaw momentarily clenching. 'Why we've exchanged vows today is nobody's business but ours. You have my word that no one will dare to question you on it.'

'Because you've decreed it?'

His eyes hardened. 'Yes.'

'And they obey whatever you say, without question?'

A spine-tingling glint flickered through his eyes. 'I'm in a unique position to demand that obedience, so, yes.'

'And how did you garner such unquestioning loyalty?' I semi-taunted, a little too eager to get beneath his skin the way he so effortlessly got beneath mine.

'By giving them what their grasping little hearts desire, of course. Isn't that the way to command most people's allegiance? Something in return for something more?'

Flint-hard bitterness glazed his words, triggering a burst of alarm.

*Something in return for something more.*

Wasn't that what my father had orchestrated for himself with his own family? A calculated means to an end?

Neo couldn't have made his endgame clearer. So why was I plagued with the urge to be sure? 'Does that apply to you too?'

The faintest ripple whispered over his jaw. 'We're not talking about me.'

'Aren't we?' I asked.

But when he started to speak, I shook my head to preempt him. To mitigate the ball of hurt that far too closely resembled the pain I'd felt at my father's actions.

'I'm not sure what happened to you to make you believe that's how everyone ticks—'

His eyes grew icily livid as he stared me down. 'I do not require your pity. Not now or ever,' he stated through gritted teeth.

Aware I'd touched on a raw nerve, I breathed in, curled my hands in my lap to stop them from reaching out for him. 'It wasn't pity. It was a need to understand—'

'Again, this isn't a lesson in dissecting my character, Sadie.'

Aware we were now drawing his parents' gaze, I took another breath. 'Fine. When will I start work?'

Scepticism and suspicion glinted in his eyes. 'So eager to get down to business?' he drawled. 'Not even time to entertain the idea of a honeymoon? You are aware that, as Mrs Xenakis, you now have the power to command my pilot to take you anywhere in the world your heart desires?'

I forced a shrug, and the uncanny sense that this was some kind of test intensified the chaos inside me. 'As tempting as that is, what's the point? We both know what this is. What *my* heart desires is to get started on my internship and finish my degree.'

The tic in his jaw returned, a little more insistent this time. 'You don't need reminding, I hope, that taking care of yourself and the baby is your number one priority?'

My fingers tightened. 'No, I don't. And you're beginning to sound like a broken record.'

'If you wish me to lay off, then have some food. It will please me,' he tossed in silkily, offering the succulent chicken again.

But my appetite had disappeared.

'If you're so interested in the chicken, Neo, then you have it. I'm going to powder my nose. And, in case you don't get that, it's a euphemism for *I need some space*.'

The briefest flare of his nostrils was the only sign he was displeased. In that moment I didn't care. I walked away, making a beeline for the wide opening of the living room wing. With the glass doors folded back and tucked out of sight, and late-afternoon sunlight spilling in through the glass ceiling onto the stylish grey and white Cycladic furnishings, the inside was a breathtaking extension of the outside.

Despite the chaos reigning inside me, I couldn't help but be affected by the stunning beauty surrounding me. But it only lasted for a minute—then reality came crashing back.

I blindly turned down one hallway, relieved when a half-open door revealed the sanctuary I was looking for. Shutting myself in, I attempted to regulate my breathing as questions ricocheted in my head.

The postcard my father left me had testified to the fact that selfishness and greed were his mainstays. But what had happened to Neo to fuel *his* actions?

Over the last week I'd given in to curiosity and done more internet searching. Very few details had been forthcoming regarding his broken engagement to Anneka. Even the circumstances of his accident were obfuscated. Although about the tall, Dutch beauty herself there'd been reams and reams, prompting in me even more questions as to why two people who'd outwardly looked like the kind of couple romance novels portrayed had parted ways.

I wanted to tell myself I didn't care. Again, my very emotions mocked me. The need to know, to see beneath the surface of the man I'd married, clawed at me.

Ten minutes dragged by. Knowing I couldn't remain hidden in the bathroom for ever, I splashed cool water over my hands, dabbed a few drops at my throat before exiting—just in time to see Callie Xenakis enter the living room, carrying baby Andreos.

She spotted me and smiled. 'I came in here to escape the heat for a few minutes. Won't you join me?' she invited, her movements graceful as she sank into one sumptuous sofa.

For some reason I hesitated, my gaze darting outside

to where Neo stood with his brother. There were similar intense expressions on their ruggedly handsome faces as they spoke.

Ax said something to Neo, his expression amused. Neo responded sharply, his mouth flattening into a displeased line which only seemed to further amuse his brother.

'Do me a favour and leave those two alone for now? Ax's been wanting payback for a while,' Callie said with a grin.

'Payback for what?'

Her stare was wickedly teasing but also contemplative, as if she was wondering whether she could trust me.

After a couple of seconds, she shrugged. 'I'm sure you've seen the papers. Let's just say my marriage didn't get off to a rosy start. And Neo… Well, he enjoyed a few jokes at his brother's expense. And those two are nothing if not competitive.'

I frowned. 'So your husband's ribbing my… Neo about me?' Somehow I couldn't bring myself to call him *my husband*.

Callie laughed. 'Ax thought he'd have to wait years to get back at his little brother. If ever.'

'I'm not sure there's much humour in any of this.'

Her eyes grew even more speculative, and there was an intelligence shining in the blue depths that made me wish for different circumstance for our meeting. I would have liked to be friends with Callie Xenakis.

'I don't think you need telling that everyone's wondering about you. This wedding came out of the blue.'

I firmed my lips, reminded of Neo's claim that our marriage was nobody's business.

As if she'd read my thoughts, Callie waved an airy hand. 'It's no one's business but yours, of course, but… Well, no one expected this from Neo. Not so fast, anyway,' she murmured, then grimaced, her gaze searching mine before she returned her attention to her son.

Sensing that she'd said more than she'd intended to, I

let the subject go, unaware that my gaze had strayed to Neo until he turned his head sharply, lanced me with those piercing eyes that threw fresh sparks of awareness over my skin. Even when his brother spoke again, Neo kept his gaze on me, the ice receding to leave a steady blaze that set off fresh fireworks.

It took monumental effort to pull my gaze free, to suck air into my lungs and turn back to Callie, who was laying her son on the wide seat, keeping one hand on his plump little belly to stop him wriggling off as she picked up a futuristic-looking remote and pressed a button.

Immediately a section of the ceiling went opaque, granting a little reprieve from the sun's rays.

As I moved towards her, her gaze flickered over my dress. 'That's a stunning dress,' she said, a wistful tone in her voice.

I stared down at my wedding gown. The style was simple, the bodice had a wide neck and capped sleeves that gave glimpses of my skin beneath the lace, and the soft layered skirt parted discreetly at intervals to show my legs when I moved. The whole ensemble felt like the softest, most seductive whisper against my skin.

'I… Thank you.'

She smiled, but a hint of sadness crossed her face before evaporating a moment later.

'Can I ask you a question?' I ventured.

'Of course,' she invited.

'What does *dikos mou* mean?'

Her eyes widened, and when she blushed I cringed inside, wondering if I'd committed a faux pas. 'I'm sorry. I didn't think it was anything rude—'

'Oh, no, it's not. It's just that Ax says it a lot. Where did you hear it?'

I bit my lip, still not certain I wanted to divulge it. 'Neo said it after…after we exchanged rings.'

A mysterious little smile played on her lips. 'It means *mine*,' she said.

'Oh…' My heart lurched in a foolish, dizzy somersault before I could remind myself that Neo's hand had been splayed over my belly when he'd said the words. That he had simply been revelling in his possession.

Nothing else.

Catching Callie's speculative glance, I hurriedly changed the subject to one I hoped would distract her: her baby. It worked like a charm—the gorgeous Andreos was almost too cute in his little shorts, shirt and waistcoat combo.

The reprieve didn't last, and the tingling along my nape alerted me that Neo had entered the room a second before my eyes were compelled to meet his. His incisive gaze raked my face as he stalked towards me, his brother a few steps behind him.

Axios made a beeline for his wife and son, catching up a giggling Andreos and tucking him against his side before he wrapped a possessive arm around his wife's shoulders.

Sliding her arm around her husband's waist, Callie said smilingly over her shoulder, 'Welcome to the family, Sadie. I have a feeling you'll find things interesting.'

Before I could ask what she meant by that, Neo closed the gap between us, one strong, lean hand held out. 'My parents are leaving. Perhaps you'd be so kind as to join me to see them off?' he enquired silkily.

That look before, as he stood next to his brother…

The terse, revealing little conversation before that…

The thought of taking his hand now…

My instincts shrieked at me to *beware*. And yet every argument as to why I shouldn't burned to ashes when his hand crept up another imperious notch.

I raised my hand.

He took it, his fingers meshing with mine in a palm sliding that jolted electricity through my midriff before spreading out in gleeful abandon over my body, hardening my nipples, speeding my heartbeat and delivering a mocking weakness to my knees.

I was fighting—and losing—the battle for my equilibrium when we stepped outside and approached Electra and Theodolus Xenakis.

Neo had inherited Theo's height and Electra's piercing eyes. Together they were a striking couple, who regarded me with shrewd speculation.

'Perhaps you and Neo would join us for dinner after you return from your honeymoon? I'd like to get to know my new daughter-in-law better,' Electra said, the barest hint of a smile diluting the near command to a request.

About to reply that there was no honeymoon, I paused when Neo answered smoothly, 'Thank you, Mama. We'll let you know when we're free.'

The tenor of his voice put paid to any more conversation. Within minutes they'd departed, followed closely by Axios and Callie.

My mother, the last one remaining, hurried to me, her face creased in smiles. 'It's been a wonderful day,' she said, and sighed. Then her smile turned teary. 'I can't believe my little girl is married,' she mused. 'If only your—'

'The helicopter's waiting, Mum,' I said hurriedly, before she could drop my father into the conversation. She'd agreed to enter rehab to deal with her gambling and the after-effects of my father's desertion. 'I'll see you when I get back to Athens.'

As for my father—I'd tried to block him out, the part of me that blamed him for contributing to my dire straits giving way to the bone-deep hurt caused by his abandonment and never healing. Even the mere thought of walking away from *my* baby filled me with horror. That he'd done so without a backward glance…

Aware of Neo's narrowed gaze on my face, I dredged up a wider smile, hugged my mother and watched her board the helicopter a minute later.

Then, in the dying rays of the sun, bar the dozen or so staff efficiently cleaning up, I was alone on a Greek island with the man I'd married.

The profundity of it hit me square in the chest. A quick glance showed he was still watching me. Still assessing me with those all-seeing eyes.

'The helicopter is coming back for us, right?'

His gaze grew hooded, his eyes flicking towards the aircraft that was now a speck on the horizon. 'Yes. But not till tomorrow evening.'

My heart stuttered and flipped. 'What? Why?'

'Because, as much as we both know why this event happened, I'd rather not fuel further speculation by spending what's left of my wedding day behind my desk in Athens with my new wife in tow.'

'I thought you didn't care what anyone thought?'

He turned, his hand returning to my waist as he led me back inside the sprawling villa. 'Everyone here today values discretion. Beyond the boundaries of that circle is another matter. You'll learn the difference in time,' he stated.

The quiet force behind his words seeped into me, drawing a shiver.

'You could've told me this before trapping me here,' I said, trying to summon irritation but only finding a bubble of hot excitement that swelled with each step I took inside the vast living room with Neo by my side. The potent whiff of his aftershave triggered a hunger deep inside.

'I thought you'd appreciate the peace and quiet.'

And those who didn't know better would imagine I was spending the night making love to my dynamic new husband?

The thought ramped up the heat inside me, making me grateful when Neo guided me past the grouping of sofas I'd used earlier to another set, facing endless lush greenery just beyond the sparkling pool, before dropping his hand.

'Sit down, Sadie. You'll better enjoy the sunset from this spot.' His voice was low, deep, if a little on the stiff side.

One of the wait staff approached and spoke to Neo in Greek. Without another word he walked away, his shoulders still tense.

Choosing to enjoy the temporary release from his overwhelming presence, and grateful to be off my feet, I kicked off my heels. I was smoothing down the floaty layers of delicate chiffon when a beam of sunlight caught the gems in the band on my finger. I'd been a little shell-shocked during the ceremony, but now I stared at the perfectly fitting diamond-encrusted platinum ring, a quiet sense of awe overcoming me.

I didn't need to be a jeweller to know the ring was near priceless. And I'd been stunned to see that Neo wore a similar band minus the diamonds. What was that supposed to prove? That he intended to take this role seriously, even though he was merely biding his time until his child was born? Or was it something else?

*You have my word there will be no other...*

My heart lurched, despite knowing I couldn't, *shouldn't* read anything into that.

I was writhing in confusion when his bold footsteps returned. I dropped my hand into my lap, sliding the weighted reminder of our wedding ceremony between the folds of chiffon just as he entered my eyeline.

He was carrying a large tray on which several platters of food had been arranged. 'You'll be so kind as not to argue with me over this again, won't you?' he enquired drolly, despite the implacable determination in his eyes.

As if he'd flipped a switch, my appetite came roaring back, the succulent scents emanating off the tray making my mouth water. 'Not this time, no.'

With a satisfied nod, he set the tray on my lap.

'I should change...'

His grey gaze swept over me, lingering at certain points

on my body, including my bare feet, and igniting the sparks higher. When his gaze returned to mine the glint had turned stormy, the sensual line of his mouth seeming fuller.

'There's no hurry. Eat first. Then I'll give you the tour.'

I polished off a portion of moussaka, then a salad with the chicken I'd rejected earlier, almost moaning at the flavours exploding on my tongue.

*Keep talking. It'll dissipate the heat threatening to eat you alive.*

'Earlier, you said you didn't care what anyone thought about our reasons for doing this. But you'll agree that, you being who you are, everyone's going to be curious about the woman you've married suddenly out of the blue?'

He gave a tight-lipped nod, his nostrils flaring slightly. 'They'll wonder if there's more than meets the eye. They'll wonder if you're pregnant. *How* you got pregnant.'

The food turned to sawdust in my mouth. 'You mean—'

'Certain members of my family know I can't produce children, yes.'

I pushed my tray away.

He firmly pushed the plate back in front of me. 'The deal was that you'd eat.'

*For the baby's sake.*

The words hung in the air between us.

I chewed. Swallowed. 'So they'll wonder if I'm a liar?'

His jaw rippled, tightened, but he shrugged. 'Only time will resolve that situation.'

*Or you could believe me...*

The words stuck in my throat, along with the next mouthful of food that suddenly refused to go down.

'The obvious workings of biology aside, why is it so hard for you to believe this baby is yours, Neo?' The question emerged before I could stop it.

'Because I'm not a man who accepts things at face value. Not anymore,' he said with cold precision. 'And I caution you against attempting to change that. You'll be wasting both your time and mine.'

That stark warning should have killed any softening towards him. Put me on the path back to unfeeling composure. Instead it mired me deeper in a quiet urgency to know why.

The urge was stemmed when Neo summoned a hovering staff member to clear away the tray. About to rise, I stopped, suppressing a shiver when his fingers brushed my inner arm.

'You haven't seen the sunset yet,' he murmured. 'Besides, I have something for you.'

I was torn between the stunning sunset unfolding outside and curiosity as to what he had for me. Neo won out. Only he was in no hurry. He nodded at the view.

I watched, awed, as the magnificent combination of orange, yellow and grey danced over the sparkling pool and the sea beyond, stretching across the horizon until it felt as if the whole world was bathed in splendid colour.

'It's breathtaking.'

'Yes,' he said simply.

The weight of his gaze remained as the minutes ticked by slowly and the sun dropped into the ocean. When I turned my head he was staring at me, that fierce light blazing in his eyes. My heart banged against my ribs.

To cover the flustering billowing inside, I cleared my throat. 'You mentioned a tour?'

He nodded, but didn't move. Simply reached into his breast pocket, extracted a small velvet box and prised it open. 'I should've given this to you earlier.'

The magnificent ring consisted of a large square diamond, with a red hue I'd never seen before, surrounded by two sloping tiers of smaller pure gems. The band was platinum, a perfect match to my wedding ring.

I was aware my jaw had dropped with stunned surprise, but I couldn't look away from the most beautiful piece of jewellery I'd ever seen.

'Do you like it?' he asked, his voice a little gruff.

I tore my gaze away to meet his, and was immediately trapped by a different sort of captivation. The *scorching* sort. 'Can I say I hate it, just so I don't have to wear it?'

One eyebrow rose. He was clearly surprised by my answer. 'I fail to see the logic,' he drawled.

'Wearing something like that in public is just inviting a mugging. Or worse.'

His lips twitched a tiniest fraction. 'Let me worry about that.' He held out his hand in silent command.

I hesitated. 'Neo…'

'Wear it, Sadie. It will invite less speculation. And it will please me.'

Perhaps it was the beautiful sunset and the food that had mellowed me. Perhaps this particular fight wasn't worth it because there was no downside to wearing one more ring when I'd already accepted another, binding me to this dynamic man who made my insides twist with forbidden yearning when I should have been shoring up my barriers at every turn.

I gave him my hand.

The act of Neo sliding another ring onto my finger felt vastly intimate, much too visceral. So much so, I'd stopped breathing by the time the band was tucked securely next to its counterpart. And was even more lightheaded when he wrapped his fingers possessively around mine and tugged me up.

'You won't need them,' he rasped, when I went to slip my feet back in my shoes.

He led me to the south wing, where every bedroom and salon was a lavish masterpiece of white and silver and more stunning than the last, and where a private cinema, study and wine cellar were filled to the brim with extravagances only obscenely wealthy men like Neo could afford.

The north wing contained fewer rooms, mainly an immense private living room dividing two master suites. Both suites were bordered by a tennis-court-sized terrace which housed a smaller semi-enclosed version of the swimming pool downstairs.

The urge to dip my bare toes into the sparkling water was too irresistible. I gave in, gasping in delight, only to look up to find Neo's gaze locked on my mouth.

He didn't look away.

Slowly, heat built to an inferno between us. Until that breathlessness invaded again, threatening to drive me to the edge of my sanity.

I stepped back from the pool, hoping to restore a level head. Because sex wasn't part of our bargain. It was the mind-altering drug that had led us here in the first place.

'So, does this island have a name?' I asked as he slowly advanced.

'Neostros,' he supplied, without taking his hooded gaze from me.

'You named your island after *yourself*? How…narcissistic.'

He shrugged off my words. 'More like the other way around. My grandfather bought this place long before I was born and he named it. My parents were vacationing here when my mother went into labour. I was born in one of the houses on the other side of the island.'

That glimpse into his early life made me yearn for more.

'Is your grandfather still alive?'

His face closed up, but not before a flash of twisted pain and bitterness marred his expression. 'No. He died of a heart attack as a direct result of attempting to dig his family out of hard times.'

Looking around me, seeing unfettered opulence at every turn, it was hard to believe that any Xenakis had ever experienced a minute's hardship. 'Hard times? How?'

Again his mouth twisted cynically. 'Another unfortunate example of someone wanting something more than they deserved. In this case it was my grandfather's overambitious business partner. He ran the business into the ground, then left my grandfather to pick up the pieces—but not before extending to him a business loan with crippling interest rates. The strain was too much for him. It broke my grandmother first. After she died… Well, it broke him.'

'From what I can tell, you come from a very large family. Didn't anyone step up to help?'

Neo lifted his hand and caught up a curl of my hair that had come loose. For a long moment I thought he wouldn't answer me, that he intended his intimate caress to swell higher between us until we drowned from it.

When his eyes eventually met mine, residual bitterness lingered, but the heat had grown. 'I don't want to talk about my family anymore. As you can see, someone did step up. Ax and I did what needed to be done to get back what we'd lost. But in doing so we were reminded over and over again that greed and avarice will push people into deplorable behaviour to the exclusion of all decency.'

I opened my mouth to refute it. His fingers left my hair to brush over my lips, stopping my words before I could speak them.

'If you seek to convince me otherwise…again, Sadie, I urge you to save your breath.'

*He's showing you his true colours. Believe him.*

'So you choose to operate from a position of bitterness and cynicism?'

A hard light glinted in his eyes momentarily before his expression grew shrewd, almost calculating. 'Don't you? Tell me what happened with your father.'

The sudden switch sent a cold shock wave through me. 'What?'

'You take pains to avoid discussing him even though he's alive. And I've deduced that he's a major reason for your mother's troubles. Why the secrecy? What did he do to you?'

I firmed my lips, refusing to be drawn into the painful

subject. But he'd answered my questions, even though it had been clear he didn't want to discuss it.

'Up until I was sixteen? Absolutely nothing. He was a decent father and I guess a good enough husband—I never heard my parents argue or even disagree about anything major.'

Neo frowned. 'What changed?'

'I came home from school one day to find my mother sobbing hysterically. When she calmed down enough to be coherent she handed me a postcard my father had sent from Venezuela. Only problem was, he was supposed to be on a business trip to Ireland.'

Strangling pain gripped my chest, stopped the flow of words for a moment. Neo's fingers trailed down my jaw to rest on my shoulder and, as weakening as it was, I took comfort from the warmth of his hand—enough to finish the sorry little tale of how my family had broken apart with a few scrawled lines on a cheery little exotic postcard.

'He basically said he didn't want to be married anymore. Didn't want to be a father, and he was never coming back. He'd already instructed his lawyers to file divorce papers. What he didn't warn us about was the fact that he hadn't kept up with the mortgage payments for over six months. Or that he'd cleared out their joint bank account. I was still absorbing the news when the bailiffs turned up two hours later with a court order and threw us out of our home.'

Neo cursed under his breath. 'Where did you go?'

'My mother had some savings. Enough to rent us a flat for a year. It would probably have gone further if...' I stopped, fresh shame and the raw anguish of laying myself bare halting my words.

His hand curled around my shoulder. 'If your mother's gambling problems hadn't started?'

I nodded. 'I got a part-time job, which lessened the financial burden. But Mum's depression grew, and she couldn't hold down a job. I think you get the picture of how things panned out eventually.'

'Did you ever hear from your father? Did he give a reason?'

Anguish welled high, consuming my insides. 'No. He stuck to his word and cut off all ties.'

Neo's lips flattened and his eyes bored into mine with a knowing look. 'So the facts speak for themselves. Wasn't he a senior-level banker?' he asked, shocking me anew with the depth of his knowledge about my life.

'Yes.'

'So he had the type of job that demanded respectability. He was fiercely competitive and ambitious, in a high-pressure job that often required cut-throat ruthlessness. Having a wife and child and a seemingly stable home served his purpose. Most likely got him up the rungs of his corporate ambition.'

'You're not telling me anything I don't know, Neo. Yes, my mother and I were just accessories he used while it suited him, then threw away when he was done. So?'

A tic rippled in his jaw, even as his thumb drew slow circles on my shoulder. Did he even know he was doing that?

'So face the facts.'

Unable to stand the waves of anguish, and that need to lean into his caress, I tugged myself out of his hold.

'Is that some sort of warning, Neo?' Had he sensed that occasional misjudged softening? Was this his way of mitigating it?

'Sadie—'

'Enough. Whatever it is you're trying to prove, save your breath. I know what type of person my father was. What type of person you are. There's no illusion on my part.'

His face tightened and he opened his mouth—most likely to challenge me.

'It's been a long day, Neo. I'd like to go to bed, if you don't mind.'

The glint in his eyes morphed, attaining that hooded, sensual potency that sparked every nerve ending to life. But with that spark came greater warning. An edging closer to that dangerous precipice of longing and softening. Wondering if that ring on his finger meant more than simple evidence of the transaction he'd brokered.

'It's your wedding night, Sadie. Surely you wish to make it a little more memorable than simply retiring to your bed at a few minutes past sunset?'

The weighted question started my heart thudding to a different beat.

'You've been at pains to remind me that this marriage is for the sake of the child I'm carrying. How I spend my time tonight is really none of your business.'

He inhaled slowly, and that animalistic aura wrapped tighter around me. 'Perhaps I wish to make it my business.'

I was struggling to stop my pulse from leaping wildly at that statement when his fingers returned to my throat, their sensual caress enthralling, like a magician conjuring up the most delicious trick.

But wasn't this an illusion? A dream from which I'd wake to disappointment?

With monumental effort I pulled away. 'We agreed that sex wasn't part of this bargain. It's an agreement I intend to stick to. Goodnight, Neo.'

I hurried away, my footsteps stumbling at the dark promise in the heavy gaze on my back. The gaze that compelled me to slow down, turn around, find out if he really meant it. If this wedding night following a wedding borne of facility could be something else.

# CHAPTER EIGHT

WHITE.

She needed to wear white every day for the rest of her life.

She was walking away from me, her ethereal dress floating about her like the purest cloud, and all I could think about was how enthralling she looked in white.

Sure, I was irritated. Unsettled by that conversation about her father. By her accusation that I wanted to hurt her by making her face the truth. I knew firsthand the consequences of burying your head in the sand.

In that moment none of it mattered except the way her hair shone like a living, breathing flame against the delicate white lace.

Maddeningly arousing.

Everything about this woman I'd married was temptation personified, urging the unschooled man closer. But I was well schooled in the sort of temptation she offered. And, as I'd accurately guessed, granting her wishes had in turn given me what I wanted.

Like Anneka and every woman I'd known, all that mattered to her was getting what she wanted in the end. I didn't doubt that if I was minded to strike another bargain she would accede to my wish to see her clad in white morning, noon and night.

Or perhaps even nothing at all?

The erection straining behind my fly cursed me for agreeing to the *no sex* rule. Why had I? Because in that moment, binding her to me in any way at all had been paramount?

My dealings with women after my failed engagement and the betrayal that followed had taught me one thing. Sex was only complicated when the parameters weren't set out explicitly. Sadie had proved herself a good negotiator. So why not negotiate on this too?

The thought of experiencing her again, of having her beneath me, that breathtaking face turned up to receive my kisses and that body between my hands, mine to pleasure and take pleasure in, powered me several steps after her before I caught myself. Stopped to stare down at the unusual weight of the band circling my finger.

The symbolism wasn't as easy to dismiss as I thought. I had a wife. One whom I suddenly felt a desperate need to bed.

No, not a sudden need. The lust I thought I'd dulled after that first time in my office had been building since she'd turned up in Athens. Since that potent realisation that she could be carrying my child.

Call me primitive, but the thought that I'd sowed a seed in her womb, against all the odds my doctors were still examining after new tests undertook last week, filled me with a sense of...*possession* I hadn't been able to shake.

I twisted the band around my finger. Would it be so unthinkable to strike another bargain, stake my true claim?

Yes, it would. Because that was the kind of bargain that came with a steep price. The Anneka-shaped kind that left only bitterness and regret in its wake.

I turned, heading away from the direction she'd taken.

Three hours later I was still pacing my suite, the tablet laid out with marketing reports and projections to be analysed abandoned in favour of fighting temptation. Fighting the invasion of Sadie Preston...no, Sadie *Xenakis*... in my brain.

And failing.

With an impatient grunt, I slid open the French doors, stepped onto the private terrace. The breeze cooled my skin but did nothing to alleviate the pressure in my groin demanding relief.

A full moon was reflected on a smooth, serene sea, a

picture of calm in direct opposition to the sensations roiling inside me.

Not only were Sadie's words echoing in my head, other observations about her kept intruding, grating like tiny pebbles on my otherwise smooth and solid belief system. Her reluctance to leave that dingy little flat. Her resistance to the lavishness and extravagance of the wedding planning, when most brides would have been rapturous at having an unlimited budget.

Most of all, her complete lack of concern that she'd be walking away with less than one percent of my wealth when I ended this marriage. That clause in the prenup had been deliberate. A ruthless little test she'd batted away without so much as a quibble.

And her bemusement when I brought it up… It had been so…*different*.

But was I seeing what I wanted to see? Repeating the same misjudgement I'd shown when I'd dismissed Anneka's obvious signs of infidelity and shameless avarice in favour of claiming the child she'd sworn was mine?

Restless feet propelled me towards the sound of water. To the pool Sadie had dipped her dainty feet in earlier, triggering awareness of yet another part of her body I found enthralling.

Thoughts of her feet evaporated when I was confronted by the more erotic vision rising from the moonlit pool.

Her back was to me, the tips of her fingers trailing through the water, and her gaze on the view as she moved towards the shallow end. She'd obviously been submerged moments before, because her hair was wet and pearlescent drops of water clung to her flawless skin.

Another few steps and the water dropped below her heart-shaped behind, revealed the bottom half of a white bikini moulding her curves and stopping my breath.

*Thee mou*, but I loved her in white…

The sizzling thought froze in my mind when she turned

fully to face the view, presenting me with her magnificent profile. If she'd looked spectacular before, now she was a bewitching goddess. At just over three months pregnant her shape hadn't altered profoundly, but signs of her state were visible in specific areas.

Her belly held the slightest curve and her breasts, lush and mouth-watering before, were fuller, more ripe. My palms burned with the need to cup them, to taste them.

A growl broke free from my throat before I could stop it.

She whirled around, one hand holding that rope of hair I wanted to wrap around my own wrist.

'Neo! I… I thought you were…'

'Asleep?' Hell, was that growly mess my voice?

She nodded a little jerkily, her gaze running over my body as I approached. Did her gaze linger below my belt? The throb there grew more insistent, propelling me even closer to the edge of the pool.

'Did I disturb you?' she asked.

'I couldn't sleep. And from the looks of it neither could you.'

A pulse leapt at her throat as her gaze travelled over me once more, her lips parting as she saw the unmistakable evidence of my arousal.

'Was I right? Does this night feel too…extraordinary to waste on sleep?'

Her head tilted up, her smooth throat bared to my hungry gaze as she swallowed. 'I don't know about extraordinary, but it's not every day a woman gets married. Or it could be I'm just getting used to this place—'

'It's not that and we both know it,' I interrupted, almost too keen to have her acknowledge what was happening.

She stared up at me, her breathing beautifully erratic, her face worshipped by moonbeams. Her fingers continued to twist that rope of hair. The whole picture of potent wantonness shattered another layer of my control.

I wanted to grab. To devour. To claim with a thoroughness that guaranteed we'd taste blissful insanity.

'Are you going to stay in there all night or are you done, Sadie?'

She shrugged lazily, drawing my attention to those decadent drops of water on her shoulder.

Two steps back and I snagged a warm towel. Held it out. 'Come out, Sadie.'

Exquisite defiance tilted her chin, long enough for me to feel the weight of her mutiny.

'Is that an order? Because, newsflash, I'm not in a mood to obey.'

We stayed like that, her gaze daring me. Then she turned her back, dived back under the water and swam two more lengths. Only then did she get out and approach me. Eyes on mine, she placed one foot on the shallow step. Then another.

Her full breasts swayed with her movement, her hips sashaying in hypnotic motions that drove spikes of lust deeper. With every inch of the body she exposed, my hunger trebled.

Wrapping the towel around her was a perfunctory move to enfold her within my arms. The smile tilting her lips screamed her triumph, stated she was in my arms because *she* wanted it.

When she wrapped her slim arms around my neck, I barely stopped myself from growling again. 'You want to know why I'm not in my bed? Why I'm out here, shattering my concentration even further and seeking peace of mind I know I won't find?'

Her gaze dropped from mine to lock on my lips.

'Because I do this to you,' she stated sultrily, rocking herself against my hardness in a way that left no doubt as to my state.

'Because you tempt me more than I've ever been tempted in my life.' I laughed, despite myself. Or perhaps because of the singular thought that it was no use fighting this. That

I didn't even want to. 'Despite my every reserve, I hunger for you.'

She inhaled, sharp and sweet, her pink tongue flicking out to swipe across her lower lip.

I captured it, bit her sensitive flesh in punishment for the cyclone of need it had created in me. When she moaned, I deepened the caress, slanted my lips over hers, claimed that mouth and satisfied a fraction of that hunger, even while it continued to rage out of control.

Tentatively, her tongue darted out to meet mine, and I took possession of it, gliding and tasting in an erotic dance I wanted to repeat all over her naked body. Especially that snug, glorious place between her legs.

Finally, I speared my fingers into the heavy mass of her damp hair to tilt her face higher, drive my kiss deeper. When she opened wider for me I couldn't stop my groan of pure satisfaction.

'Your hair is a work of art, *pethi mou*. Simply exquisite.'

'Neo…'

I backed us up a few steps, until the terrace wall met her back and the soft cushion of her body moulded my front.

'And this mouth. *Christos*, you have the most divine mouth,' I confessed, rediscovering that sensitive spot in her neck where her pulse throbbed before returning to reclaim her mouth. 'I haven't been able to stop thinking about kissing you since that unsatisfactory sampling at the altar.'

My free hand slid down her body, stopping briefly to mould one plump, mouth-watering breast, before travelling lower, to cup her hot feminine centre.

'Haven't stopped thinking about this special place either. Imagining you wrapped tight around me again, taking me inside you.'

She whimpered against my lips. 'I… I shouldn't be doing this,' she murmured, almost to herself.

*And I shouldn't crave you this much. And yet here I am…*

Through the damp material of the bikini bottom I caressed her, my thumb circling that engorged bead I craved to have between my lips. When the need grew beyond containment I slipped my fingers beneath the stretchy fabric. Touched her where I needed to touch her.

Her knees sagged and she whimpered again. Muttered words against my lips I was too incoherent to absorb.

Which was why it took a moment to realise that the hand curled around my wrist, and the other flat against my chest, were both attempting to push me away.

'Neo…we can't…'

The protest was feeble, the look on her face as I drew back a touch torn between hunger and rebellion.

I fought the voracious need gripping me and started to withdraw my hand.

Her thighs clamped around it, holding me prisoner.

'You say we can't while looking at me with yearning in your eyes. Your body clings to mine while you deny me what I want. What we both want. You think I don't feel how wet you are for me, Sadie?'

Heat rushed into her face. Her thighs parted with an abrupt jerk and she swiftly dropped her hands. 'This… It's just chemistry.'

'There's no such thing as "just chemistry." Especially not when it's this powerful. When it creates this response.'

My gaze dropped tellingly to the tight furling of her nipples, clearly visible against the damp bikini top.

'It means nothing,' she protested. 'Besides, sex is what got us here in the first place!'

The cold compress of her words washed away a layer of blazing arousal. 'And it's a place you don't wish to be? Is that it?'

'Don't put words in my mouth. I may not have been prepared for this baby but I've vowed to give it the best life possible. That doesn't mean I want to mess up my life with sex. So if you're looking for a way to scratch your itch you'll…' She stopped, her throat moving as she swallowed her words.

'I'll what, Sadie?'

She shook her head, sending wet tendrils flying. I caught a strand, tucking it behind one ear. Her pulse jumped beneath my touch.

'You can't say the words, can you?' I taunted, deriving a little devilish satisfaction from it. 'Did you fool yourself into thinking giving me liberties I didn't want would be easy?'

She turned her face to the side, avoiding my gaze. 'I don't know what you're talking about.'

My grating laughter earned me a ferocious glare. I caressed her cheek, unable to resist touching her even now. 'Do you not? Really? Then let me posit a theory. Perhaps this marriage isn't as clinical as you wish it to be? Perhaps this itch you speak of isn't a one-sided thing?'

Watching her gather her frayed composure was a thing of unwanted awe.

'I'm a grown woman, Neo. With independent thoughts and needs I can choose to indulge or deny. While the last few minutes have been pleasant, it's not worth sullying my life for. So, no, the itch will remain a one-sided thing and no amount of temptation will sway me. Goodnight.'

For the second time I watched her walk away from me, leaving even more chaos behind. Acknowledging that I wanted her much more than I'd wanted any other woman in my life, that I might never have her, disarmed me enough to leave me propped up against the wall long after she and her voluptuous curves and her stubborn defiance had disappeared behind her suite doors.

But when the realisation hit that I, Neo Xenakis, was being denied a woman's attention for the first time in my life, I surged away from that wall, determined to rid myself of this…infernal need.

A teeth-gritting, bracing cold shower restored a little sanity. But with sanity came the acknowledgement that perhaps I hadn't bargained as well as I'd thought for what I wanted.

Because what I wanted was…*more*.

And nothing drove home that realisation harder than the first prenatal scan just days later.

When I heard the strong, powerful heartbeat of my child for the first time.

I couldn't look away from the unrestrained stamp of possession on Neo's face and that flash of uncertainty and apprehension as he stared at the monitor. I might have serious doubts as to his motives in other things, but in this I couldn't dismiss the strength of his feelings. But were they positive? Or calculated?

As the doctor took measurements and studiously recorded details, Neo's gaze drifted feverishly over my face, then down my body to latch onto my belly.

*'Dikos mou,'* he murmured, with even more fervour than he had two days ago.

*Mine.*

That proclamation moved something in me, and I was glad for the echo of my baby's heartbeat otherwise I was sure he'd have heard my own thundering heart.

Would it be the end of the world to give in to this unrelenting craving?

The thought wasn't easy to dispel, especially now, when he leaned closer, his body bracing mine on the king-sized bed.

Like a flower reaching for the sun, my every cell strained for him, defiantly ignoring my inner protests.

It was almost a relief when the doctor finished the scan and printed off two copies, which Neo immediately took possession of, sliding one into his wallet and handing me the other.

When I reached for it he held on to it for a moment, his eyes pinning mine as his fingers brushed my skin. Something heavy and intense fired up in his eyes—something that should have sent apprehension dancing down my spine but instead left molten heat in my belly, my heartbeat fast enough to match my baby's.

The moment passed.

After Neo's rapid-fire questions provided reassurance that the baby was healthy, the doctor and his technician were dismissed and Neo turned to me.

'How do you feel?' he asked.

'Well enough to start work.'

His mouth compressed and I geared myself for another disagreement.

'The morning sickness has passed?'

I nodded. 'It stopped about a week ago.'

His gaze returned to my belly, stayed for fevered seconds. 'Very well. We'll leave in half an hour.' With brisk strides, he left the room.

I rose, spinning slowly in place, still awed by my surroundings. By the size of the bedroom that would easily fit my previous home twice over. Not to mention the dressing room.

I approached the large, cavernous room decked from floor to ceiling in wood, and tastefully arranged into sections for shoes, handbags, day and evening wear.

Last night, when the helicopter landed in the exclusive neighbourhood of Voula, minutes from the centre of Athens, I'd been too overwhelmed by the hour spent in close proximity to Neo to appreciate the opulence of his tiered mansion.

Unsurprisingly, every square inch dripped with luxury. Cream with grey-veined marble and hues of dark blue and grey was the theme running through each room. Set into its own vast exclusive hillside, it overlooked a miles-long vista, with the Acropolis the jaw-dropping centre of attraction.

The staff of six spoke impeccable English, and after I'd dressed, the housekeeper directed me to Neo's study.

My knock was answered in deep, crisp tones. When I entered his gaze was hooded, loaded with the sort of heavy speculation and calculation that sent another wave of sensation over my skin.

I'd walked away on Saturday night believing that I'd ended that dangerous episode before it had blown up. But with each look, I got the uncanny sensation that we weren't done. That Neo's machinations were merely gathering pace.

Which made walking beside him on the way to his underground garage a monumental task in composure keeping for me. But once we were seated in the black Maserati, the powerful engine speeding us through early-morning traffic, he was all business.

He indicated the stylish briefcase in the footwell next to my feet. 'The briefcase is yours—so is the tablet inside it. I've loaded three marketing reports on it. I want your thoughts on them by midday.'

I grabbed the case, hung on to it as if it would dilute his effect on me.

It didn't even come close.

Our previous interactions had given me a taster of Neo's power, but my introduction to his corporate life provided a mind-bending main course of the sheer formidable force he wielded. For example, the middle-aged woman I'd encountered in his office months ago was one of six assistants poised to answer his every demand.

And his first demand was to have her summon his top marketing executives into his office, where I was introduced as his wife and personal intern—a statement that garnered speculation and brought a warm flush to my face.

But it was his second demand—that I be set up in one corner of his vast office—that drew a protest from me. 'Aren't you worried about whispers of nepotism?'

One eyebrow lifted. 'Not even a little bit,' he tossed away. At my frown he added, 'I don't intend to make this an easy ride for you, Sadie. But by all means, if you're worried about it, then prove them wrong.'

* * *

In the three dizzying weeks that followed it was impossible not to meet that challenge, to smash it to pieces. Because, while Neo was maddeningly rabid in ensuring I was provided with mouth-watering meals at precise intervals during the day, that my prenatal vitamins were taken like clockwork and my every comfort was catered for, business-wise he was a slave-driver—often lounging back in his thronelike seat while firing questions at me from across the room. He tossed every menial marketing task at me, barely letting me catch my breath before the next project landed on my desk.

And when he wasn't doing that, his gaze rested on me with molten, unapologetic interest.

It was on one such occasion, when I was feeling mellowed from a client's high praise of a marketing analysis I'd put together, that I caught his gaze on me as I rose from my desk.

'What are you thinking?' I asked, before I could curb my curiosity.

The question seemed to startle him. Then his long lashes swept over me. 'White.'

'Pardon me?'

'White suits you. You should wear only that from now on.'

An anticipatory shiver fired through me, because he'd just tossed one of his imperious observations at me. And, oh, how I'd relish batting it away.

'Is this where you say "Jump" and hope I'll say, "Yes, sir…how high do you wish, sir?"'

For some absurd reason his lips twitched with amusement. 'I'd say yes, but we both know you'd never do anything that accommodating. Not without something in return, at least.'

A pang of hurt caught me unawares.

His gaze sharpened on my face, then he grew irritated.

'That was meant to be a compliment, Sadie, not a prelude to a fight. You look beautiful in white.'

'Is that why my wardrobe is suddenly full of white stuff?' The predominantly white outfits had appeared suddenly, with no explanation offered.

He shrugged. 'I was told you didn't seem interested in the whole clothes-shopping process back in London. I made the choice for you. If I was wildly inaccurate, then feel free to amend it.'

Mutiny rose and died almost as soon as my fingers drifted over the soft white cotton dress I'd picked for the office today. The boat-necked A-line design draped over my body without clinging, cleverly disguising the small swell of my belly. And, like this dress, every item in my new wardrobe was a perfect fit.

'It's okay, I suppose.'

He inclined his head in an imperious nod, but not before I caught a look of...*relief*?

Before I could be sure, he was rising, messing with my breathing as he sauntered around to perch on the edge of his desk.

'Come here, Sadie,' he commanded, his voice gravel rough.

'Why?'

His eyes shadowed. 'Because it's time to go over the final details before our meeting,' he said easily.

I wasn't fooled. The fierce gleam in his eye announced other intentions.

But, unable to resist that hypnotic voice, I stumbled over to him. He caught my hips between his hands, positioning me between his spread legs, and as he stared down into my face I struggled to catch my breath. And then the most wondrous thing happened.

I felt the sweetest, most delicate tingling in my belly.

'Oh!'

His gaze sharpened. 'What is it?'

'I just felt…'

Raw, thick emotion arrested his face. 'The baby?'

The hushed gravity of his voice, the depth of yearning in his voice, disarmed me.

'According to all indications you *should* be experiencing the first movements of my child inside you,' he rasped.

'I thought I felt something…a flutter yesterday…but it hasn't happened again—' The fluttering came again, making me gasp. 'Oh!'

His gaze dropped to my belly, and his hand slowly lowered to hover over the small bump. 'I would very much like to touch you, Sadie,' he said, his voice gravel rough.

Shakily fighting back hormonal tears, I nodded. He exhaled raggedly, his warm hand remaining on me for long moments, during which the fluttering was repeated twice more, each time drawing from him an awed gasp.

Stormy eyes rose to mine. 'I said you looked beautiful. That wasn't quite accurate. You look radiant.' One hand rose to caress my cheek. 'Your skin glows with exquisite vitality. I've never quite seen anything like it.'

'It's…it's the pregnancy. Not me.'

'Most women would wholeheartedly bask in such a compliment, but not you,' he murmured, his gaze curiously flummoxed. 'Are you so determined to topple my opinion of you?' he rasped, a touch disgruntled.

'Neo—'

'Hush, *pethi mou*. Let us enjoy this moment,' he suggested, his voice hypnotic.

We stood trapped in that intensely soul-stirring bubble until the ringing phone made us both jump. I hastily stepped back from the exposing moment.

Back to a reality where this pregnancy was the sole reason I had a ring on my finger and a place in Neo's office.

Back to a place where the softening emotions that had been expanding over the past few weeks needed to be shoved back into a box marked *delusional*.

When he reached over to answer his phone I escaped, reciting every reason why resisting temptation and Neo was essential to my equilibrium.

When I returned, half an hour later, Neo's laser-beam eyes focused on the frosted treat in my hand. 'What's that?'

I raised an eyebrow. 'It's a cupcake, Neo.'

'I can see that. I meant *that*.' He pointed his arrogant nose at the thin candle perched in the middle of the frosting.

'It's a candle. Which I'm going to light when I get to my desk and then blow out. Because it's my birthday.'

He went pillar still. 'What did you say?'

'I said it's my birthday today.'

His eyes narrowed. 'If this is a ploy of some sort—'

'You think I'd bother to lie about something you can find out in less than ten seconds?'

The fire and brimstone left his eyes immediately, leaving him looking curiously nonplussed.

'Wow. So much for me thinking felicitations might be forthcoming,' I said.

My waspish tone further unnerved him. Then his lips firmed.

'You scurried away before we were done talking. You do realise you're not doing yourself any favours by annoying me, don't you?'

I shrugged. 'I'm here now, and I don't see a fire, so…'

His eyes widened a fraction, then I caught a hint of amusement. Again I had the feeling that the mighty Neo Xenakis liked being challenged.

Striding over, he took the cupcake from me, set it on my desk and took my hand.

'What are you doing? And, more importantly, why are you separating me from my cupcake?'

He frowned, or least gave an impression of it. But it fell far short of his overriding expression—bewilderment. Perhaps even a little shame.

'You asked where the fire was. Our meeting has been rescheduled to now.'

'What? But—'

'You helped the team land the deal that has brought the Portuguese trade minister here. I don't think you'll want to keep him waiting while you devour a dubious-looking confection from a vending machine.'

'It wasn't from a vending machine. It was from your executive restaurant, which is manned by a chef I hear is on the brink of winning his first Michelin star.'

He simply shrugged and kept moving while he extracted his phone from his pocket. Rapid-fire Greek greeted whoever answered the call, after which he held open the door to the conference room with one eyebrow hiked up.

'You know there's a rule against keeping a pregnant woman from what she craves, don't you?'

My words had been meant harshly. Instead they emerged in a sultry undertone, wrapped in a yearning that was only partly for the cupcake he'd forced me to abandon.

And if I had any doubt that my words had triggered the same thought in him, the darkening of his eyes and the slight parting of his sensual mouth told me we'd skated away from the subject of cupcakes to something more potent.

'I will bear the consequences of it this once,' he rasped, his voice an octave lower. Deeper.

*Sexier.*

My gaze dropped to the sensual line of his lips and I sucked in a breath.

'The minister is waiting, Sadie. As much as I want to answer that look in your eyes, it won't do for me to start making love to my wife in full view of a potential business associate.'

*My wife.*

It was the first time he'd referred to me as that since the wedding…

The two-hour meeting passed in a rush of effectively

troubleshooting every last one of the minister's objections. While the team acted in perfect cohesion, Neo seemed intent on lobbing further questions for me to answer, giving a satisfied nod when I did.

Perhaps he wanted to give me a chance to prove my worth, to publicly expunge any hint of nepotism once and for all. Whatever the reason, it left me with a warm, buoyant glow that shrivelled the hard knot of unworthiness that had clung to me and drew a wide smile once the minister left, satisfied.

Perhaps my smile was too wide. Too proud. It certainly triggered something in Neo, and his stride was purposeful as he marched me from the conference room.

'I hate to repeat myself, but where's the fire?' I asked.

'I'm giving you the rest of the day off,' he declared.

'I can't take time off *and* finish the work you've asked me to do.'

He merely shrugged as he stepped with me into the lift and pressed the button for the parking garage, where a valet stood next to his car, keys ready.

'Change of plan,' Neo said, once I was seated and he'd slid behind the wheel. 'There's an event I need you to attend with me tonight.'

'Oh? Do you want to tell me about it so I can prepare?'

While the thought of working on my birthday hadn't disheartened me, because working with Neo was a secret thrill I wouldn't pass up, I wasn't sure I wanted to be thrown into the deep end of an unknown situation.

'Preparation won't be necessary,' he said cryptically. 'But dress formally.'

For the rest of the journey back to the villa he fell into silence, his profile not inviting conversation.

Inside, he excused himself, shutting his study door behind him with a definitive click.

I retreated to my dressing room to face the daunting task of picking what to wear. Eventually, I chose a white gown made of the softest tulle layered over satin. The gathered material swept down from one shoulder and cupped my bust before falling away in a long, elegant sweep to my ankles. I complemented it with light, champagne-coloured strappy heels and a matching clutch, and left my earlobes and throat free—simply because the jewellery I owned was too understated for the gown, and because I still had no clear idea of where Neo was taking me.

As if I'd conjured him up, his firm knock arrived.

I opened the door and suppressed a gasp.

His business suit had been swapped for a dinner suit, a dark silk shirt, a darker-hued tie and bespoke shoes polished to within an inch of their life. With his freshly showered hair slicked back, and his face and that cleft in his chin thrown into relief, it was all I could do to not stare open-mouthed at the overwhelmingly dashing figure he cut.

His return scrutiny was electric, his eyes turning a skin-tingling stormy grey as they sizzled over my body. 'You look exquisite,' he pronounced, managing to sound arrogant and awed at the same time.

The combination melted me from the inside out, and my heart was pounding even before he held out his arm in silent invitation.

I slid my hand into the crook of his elbow, concentrated in putting one foot in front of the other as he led me not to the garage but out through the wide living room doors and down another terrace towards the helipad.

He helped me into the sleek aircraft, then strapped himself in.

'Are you going to tell me where we're going?' I asked.

He slanted me a lazy, shiver-inducing glance. 'You'll see for yourself in a few minutes.'

The aircraft lifted off, flew straight towards the horizon for a full minute, then started to descend again. When it banked slightly to the right to land, I saw it.

The Acropolis.

Lit to magnificent perfection, it was a breathtaking sight to behold. 'We're meeting the client *here*?'

Neo simply gave an enigmatic smile, deftly alighted when the aircraft set down, and held out his hand to me. I'd been in Athens long enough to know that tours took place both day and night. But there was no one around— just a handful of dark-suited men, one of whom looked suspiciously like… *Wendell*.

A sharp glance at Neo showed that enigmatic expression still in place.

My heart thundered harder.

At the Parthenon, I wanted to linger, the beauty surrounding me demanding appreciation. But Neo's fingers tightened.

'You can have a private tour later, if you wish. But not now.'

I discovered why minutes later, felt something sacred break away and hand itself over to Neo without my approval or permission. Because there was no event. No client. Just an elaborately laid candle-lit table set for two in the middle of the Temple of Athena Nike.

Emotion, far too delicate and precious for this man who could be in equal parts hard and bitter and magnetic, swelled inside me. 'Neo, why are we here?'

He stepped forward, drew back my chair. 'You helped land a very big deal for Xenakis today. An achievement worth celebrating,' he said.

And as that warm bubble of *worthiness* expanded inside me, he added, 'Plus, it's your birthday.'

My throat clogged, dangerously happy emotions brimming.

'I spoke to your mother's counsellor at the rehab centre. She didn't think it would be wise to grant dispensation for your birthday. *Syngnómi*. I'm sorry.'

'It's fine. I'm just glad she's getting the help she needs.'

Deep down, while I'd have loved to share this moment

with her, I was selfishly glad I had this all to myself. That I had Neo all to myself, as unwise as the thought was.

It took a few minutes for the shock to wear off, to grasp the fact that he'd had the tours shut down, had his executive chef prepare a sublime meal and transported it to this incredible place. All in a handful of hours.

The impact of his actions threatened to drown me in dangerous emotion. The kind that prompted yearnings that would never be fulfilled. The kind that led to restless, need-filled nights.

In a bid to put some distance between myself and those feelings, I glanced at pillars that whispered with history. 'Was Athena Nike not a fertility goddess?'

Neo inclined his head, his gaze brooding. 'Which makes this location apt, does it not?'

A blush crept into my cheeks, and when his gaze lingered boldly, heat spread fast and hard over my body.

Easy conversation flowed between us as we ate. And when the pièce de résistance was wheeled out—an enormous cupcake-shaped birthday cake, with a single candle set into the pink frosting—I fought back tears as Neo took my hand and led me to it.

'You made a wish?' His tone suggested the idea was alien to him.

'I did. Something wrong with that?' I asked when an involuntary muscle clenched in his jaw.

'Wishes are useless. Reality is what matters.'

Bruising hurt launched itself into my chest. 'It's my birthday. I'm one hundred percent sure you're not allowed to rain on my birthday parade.'

He stared at me for a long spell. Then nodded abruptly. '*Ne*, I'm not. What I *can* do is give you your birthday gift.'

From his pocket, he pulled a sleek, oblong box. Before he could open it, I laid my hand over his.

'I don't need a present, Neo. This…' I waved my hand at the setting '…is more than enough.'

He blithely ignored me and flicked the box open.

Inside nestled a gorgeous necklace. Fiery ruby stones battled with sparkling diamonds for radiance. I couldn't help my gasp.

'You might not want a gift, but it's yours nevertheless,' he stated, in that absolute manner I'd come to accept was simply his nature.

'And you want me to take it because it will please you?' I semi-mocked, using his words from before.

He shook his head. 'Because it will look beautiful on you. Because the rubies match your sensational hair and it would be a shame to keep this thing in a box.'

The compliments burrowed deep inside me, disarming me long enough for him to fasten the necklace, step back and boldly admire it.

'You have a thing for my hair, don't you?' I said.

Expecting a mocking comeback, my heart flipped over when raw need tightened his face.

Before I could draw a breath he was capturing my shoulders, dragging me against his body. 'I have a thing for *you*, Sadie. For all of you,' he breathed, right before his head swooped down.

Helpless to deny the hunger which had been building inside me for weeks, I surged onto my toes and met his fiery kiss. Sensation went from one to one hundred in the space of a heartbeat. In a tangle of limbs we grappled to get closer, to kiss deeper, to sate an insatiable need.

When an abstract sense of propriety finally drove us apart, we were both breathing harshly, and Neo's face was a taut mask of arousal. His hands continued to roam over my body, stoking need, until I feared my heart would bang clean out of my ribcage.

Lips parted in stunned surprise, I watched him sink to his knees, frame my hips between his hands, before leaning forward to kiss the swell of my belly. When he rose again, his eyes churned with thunder and lightning, his hands trailing fire when he cupped my nape and angled my face to his.

'I want you, Sadie. Naked. In my bed, beneath me. Think of the sublime pleasure I can give you and give in to me,' he coaxed, his fingers caressing my throat.

My knees sagged, the heady words finding their target and weakening my resolve. I scrambled hard for it. Because when it came right down to it, what Neo was offering was great sex. But still only sex.

I wanted more. Much more than I'd even allowed myself to dream of.

It was that very monumental need that made me shake my head. 'I can't. Not for a quick tumble that will simply complicate things. Besides, this isn't part of our agreement.'

*And it's not enough for me.*

His face slowly hardened. 'Be careful, Sadie, that you don't box yourself into a corner you'll regret.'

Those cryptic words stayed with me long after we'd returned to the villa. Long after he'd bade me a curt goodnight and left me at the door of my suite.

Undressing, I caught sight of myself in the mirror and gasped, the effect of the spectacular necklace freezing me in place. I couldn't help but appreciate its beauty. Appreciate the compliments Neo had paid me. Dwell on the look in his eyes before he'd kissed me.

*I have a thing for you...all of you...*

Had I dismissed his words too quickly? Had he been paving the way for...*more*?

A glance at my bedside clock showed it was only just past ten. My birthday wouldn't be over for another two hours.

Perhaps it wasn't too late to make another wish come true.

# CHAPTER NINE

I TOSSED THE covers aside and slid out of bed before I lost my nerve.

My knock on his door elicited a sharp, gruff response. My clammy hand turned the handle and, ignoring my screaming senses telling me to turn back, I nudged it open.

He was reclined in the middle of his emperor-sized bed, his top half bare and his lower half covered by a dark green satin sheet. For several heartbeats he stared at me, a tight expression on his face.

'Come to drive a few more points home?' he asked eventually, his voice taut.

Unable to clear the lump of nerves lodged in my throat, I shook my head.

Slowly, torturously, his gaze roved over my body, lingering at my throat, where the necklace still rested, then my breasts, hips, down my legs, before rising to stop where the hem of my silk night slip ended high on my thighs.

He swallowed hard before his gaze clashed with mine, a turbulence percolating there that triggered a similar chain reaction in me.

'Then what *do* you want, Sadie?' His accent had thickened, throbbing with deep, dark desire.

'What you said, back on Neostros, about me giving you liberty you didn't want to take. What did you mean by that?'

That mask twisted with flint-hard warning. 'Whether you end up in my bed or not, I don't plan to stray. Earlier tonight I thought we could, in time, get to a place where the possibility of renegotiating wasn't unthinkable.'

*In time...*

Once he was certain the baby I carried was his?

I forced myself to focus as he continued.

'But you shut that down, so I'm not sure why you're here. One thing you should know, though. I abhor infidelity of any sort. If that's what you're here to propose—'

'No!' My heart twisted with dark, rabid jealousy. 'That wasn't… That's not why I'm here.'

'Spit it out, my sweet. There's only so much torture I'll take from my wife. Even on her birthday. Especially when she's standing there looking like my every fantasy come to life.'

His gaze dropped again, this time to the fingers I was unconsciously twisting in front of me. Something eased in his eyes and he reared up from his recline.

At the sight of his sculpted chest, my mouth dried. Then almost immediately flooded with a hunger that weakened me from head to toe.

'Come here, Sadie,' he commanded gruffly.

I shook my head. 'You're going to have to come and get me.'

Expecting an arrogant comeback, I was surprised when his jaw clenched and his fingers bunched on the sheets. For an age, he contemplated me, his gaze weighing mine.

If I hadn't known better I'd have imagined Neo was… *nervous.*

Before the thought could deepen, he swung his legs over the side of the bed and rose.

And for the first time I saw Neo naked. Saw him in his full magnificent glory.

Saw the deep, stomach-hollowing scars that dissected his left hip, then zigzagged their way over his pelvis to end dangerously close to his manhood.

My hand shot up to my mouth, a horrid little gasp escaping me before I could stop it.

Dear God, so *that* was why he believed he couldn't have children?

Neo's head jerked back, his eyes darkening at my reaction. Yet he didn't flinch or cower. Hell, he seemed resolute, even a little proud to show off his scars. He prowled forward, naked and unashamed, his impressive manhood at full mast.

'What's the matter, Sadie?' he rasped when he was a handful of feet away. 'Is this too much for you? Are you going to run from me? Again?'

My gaze flew to his. 'No! What would make you think that?'

His eyes shadowed and he paused for several beats. 'The sight of me doesn't horrify you?' he asked, a peculiar note in his voice.

'Of course I'm not horrified. I'm heartsick that you had to endure that. Who wouldn't be?'

His lips twisted bitterly. 'I've discovered from past…encounters…that there are three reactions to my scars. Horror, pity or stoicism.'

'Well, I don't belong in any of those groups, thank you very much.'

Again his gaze probed mine. 'Do you not?'

'No. And if you keep looking at me like that I'll leave right now.'

'Your words salve me a little…but perhaps I require more? A demonstration of why you're in this room in the first place?' he said huskily. 'If you're not here to torture me, *pethi mou*, then why are you here?'

His voice grew more ragged, his chest rising and falling along with the impressive arousal that was somehow growing even prouder by the second.

I dragged my gaze from his intoxicating body. 'I came to tell you that I've changed my mind. That I… I want…'

God, what a time to be struck senseless. But, really, who could blame me? When he looked this magnificent? When it seemed—powerfully and thrillingly—that I had this effect on him?

'I want the fantasy,' I whispered.

'What fantasy? Tell me what you want, Sadie. Explicitly.'

Nerves ate harder, knotting my tongue.

'Perhaps it would be better to show me, hmm?' he encouraged, his voice a barely audible rasp.

Had he said this with even a stitch of clothing on I would have balked. But with the miles of gleaming olive skin on show, his virility just begging to be explored and every atom in my body screaming for contact, the urge was impossible to deny.

My twitching hands flexed, rose. Brushed over one long, thin, jagged scar.

A sharp breath hissed out.

I snatched my hand away. 'I'm s-sorry. I didn't mean to hurt you.'

He gave a sharp shake of his head. 'It doesn't pain me, Sadie. Quite the opposite,' he grated.

My gaze darted to his face. While his expression was tight with barely leashed control, his eyes blazed with an emotion I couldn't quite name.

'I've never permitted anyone to explore me this way,' he added.

'Really?' Why did that please me so much?

'*Ne*. Continue. Please,' he urged.

Encouraged, I trailed my fingers over the raised skin, tracing the map of his trauma, a little in awe that he'd survived what had to have been a horrific experience.

When I neared his groin the sculpted muscles in his abs tensed, but he didn't stop me. Growing bolder, I stepped into his force field, felt the searing heat of his skin blanket me.

'Will you tell me what happened?' I asked.

He regarded me for several heartbeats, then nodded. 'Later. Much later.' Then, grasping my hand, he growled, 'Don't stop.'

The invitation was too heady to resist.

I explored him from chest to thigh, but avoided the powerful thrust of his erection until, with a growl, he swung me into his arms and strode for the bed.

Laying me down, he divested me of the slip and panties but left the necklace on. Then he stayed by the side of the bed, staring down at me with blazing eyes.

'Our first time was rushed. Understandably chaotic. This time I intend to take my time, learn everything you like. Show you what I desire. Are you willing, *pethi mou*?'

I nodded jerkily, aware that my pulse was racing at my throat.

'Good.'

Boldly, he reached forward and cupped one breast, while the other hand covered the damp heat gathering between my legs. His eyes devoured my every expression as I arched into his touch.

'I want to watch you drown in pleasure. I want to see your beautiful green eyes when you come for me.'

He toyed with one peaked nipple, drawing from me a breathless gasp, then swooped down, twirled his tongue around the tight nub, drew it into his mouth for several hot seconds before he raised his head.

'I want to hear your breath hitch like that when you lose your mind for me.'

His thumb found the needy pearl of my core and rubbed with an expertise that arched my back, made desperate moans erupt from my throat.

'Ah, just like that, *moro mou*.'

'Neo, you're making me... I'm...'

'Give yourself over to me, Sadie,' he grated thickly, urgently. 'Give me what I want and I'll reward you.'

'With...what?' I gasped.

An arrogant smile curved his sensual lips. 'With as much of me as you can take. Would you like that?'

'Yes!'

'Then come for me. Now, Sadie,' he demanded throatily, his clever fingers demanding that ultimate response as his due.

With mindless abandon I handed it over, sensation piling high as he flipped the switch that triggered my release. My screams scraped my throat raw, my body twisting in a frenzied bliss I never wanted to end.

All the while Neo rained kisses and praise on my body, his lips and hands prolonging my pleasure until I was spent. Until all I could do was try to catch my breath as he finally climbed onto the bed, parted my thighs and situated himself above me, arms planted on either side of my shoulders.

Even as my heart raced from one climax, need built again, and the sight of Neo, this powerful mountain of a man whose scars only served to make him even more unique, more potent and desirable, and yet so dangerous to my emotional well-being, rendered me speechless.

Eyes frenzied with need scoured me from head to toe. 'Touch me, Sadie,' he rasped.

Too far gone to resist, I cupped his jaw, gloried in the sharp stubble that pricked my skin, delighted when he turned his face deeper into my touch. I explored him with the same thoroughness with which he'd explored me, until his breaths turned ragged and his stomach muscles clenched with the tightness of his control.

Throwing my legs wider, I let my gaze find his. Our visceral connection thickening the desire arching between us, he surged sure and deep, filling me in places that went beyond the physical. Because as Neo began to move, a kind of joy filled my heart. One that prickled my eyes and made me cling tighter, cry out a little louder.

Because while it was wondrous it was also terrifying, this feeling. Because in those moments when sweat slicked from his body to mine, when he fused his lips to mine with a heavy, passionate groan and stepped off the edge with me, as I touched his scar and felt his pain echo in my heart, I knew this would never, ever be about just sex for me.

When it was over, when I was exhausted but sated, my hand traced the whorls of raised scar tissue, my heart squeezing as I thought of what he'd suffered.

'So was it a helicopter crash or a ski accident? The papers couldn't seem to decide on one or the other,' I said.

He stiffened, then gave a bitter chuckle. 'When have they ever bothered about what's the truth and what isn't?' Silence reigned for a handful of seconds before he added tightly, 'It was on a black run in Gstaad. A run I'd skied many times before. But familiarity and expertise don't mean a thing if there's a lack of concentration.'

I frowned. Neo wasn't the type to court danger by being reckless. The ruthless efficiency with which he'd steered events from the moment he'd learned of his child was testament to the fact that he didn't drop the ball. *Ever.*

Unless... 'Something happened?'

Grim-faced, he unconsciously tightened his hand on my hip. Not enough to hurt, but enough to signal that whatever memory I'd roused wasn't pleasant.

'The company had just started a major international push when Anneka and I got together. She was part of the ski season crowd who worshipped the slopes. I didn't mind so much when she chose to party with her friends without me. But when she told me she was pregnant—'

He stopped at my shocked gasp. 'Your fiancée was *pregnant*?'

His face turned even grimmer, his jaw clenching tight before he nodded abruptly. 'But I began to suspect that she was chasing more than prime snow when she was away.'

'She was cheating on you?'

'I sensed she wasn't being truthful about a few things. But she denied it and I...' His jaw clenched tight for a single moment. 'I chose to believe her. She convinced me to let her stay in Gstaad for a few more days before coming back to Athens. On the morning I was supposed to leave, she wanted to ski on the black run. She was an excellent skier, but she was pregnant with my child and I didn't feel right about letting her go alone. So I went with her. It started snowing heavily almost immediately. I lost sight of Anneka for a moment and lost my concentration.'

He stopped.

'I woke up from a coma three weeks later. Just in time to hear her plotting with her lover about how they would pass off their child as mine long enough to get a ring on her finger and all of my wealth. Within minutes I had no child, a duplicitous fiancée and the dreadful news that my injuries had ended any hope of my ever fathering a child naturally.'

As I was grappling with that, his turbulent gaze found mine.

'Do you understand now why hearing you'd destroyed my one last chance prompted my reaction?'

His stark bitterness threw ice-cold dread over me, keeping me numb for a minute before sensation piled in, puzzles slid into place.

With a horrified gasp I moved away from him, pulling the sheet tight around me. I suppressed another sharp cry as pain lanced me and the weighted certainty that another woman's transgressions had been the measuring rod I'd been judged against all along froze me from the inside out.

'So I'm Project Two Point Zero?'

He frowned. 'Excuse me?'

'You thought I was lying when I said I was pregnant. Then you accused me of trying to foist another man's child on you. Then you thought you'd hedge your bets by marrying me, on the off-chance the child was yours. How are those imagined offences of mine any different from what your fiancée did to you?'

He reared up, his face tightening further. 'For one thing, we're married. And for another, you barely touch the possessions I've showered on you. You don't drive, or ask to be driven anywhere. The thought of going to a social event makes you grimace.'

'So my saving grace is that I'm not a fashion whore and nor do I salivate over the dozen supercars you store in your garage? What makes you think I'm not just biding my time, lulling you into a sense of complacency before I strike?'

One insolent eyebrow rose, as if the idea was amusing. 'Are you? And how do you propose to do that?'

'Give me time—I'm sure I can come up with something.'

'You won't,' he parried arrogantly. 'You want to know how you're different?'

I pressed my lips together, the strong need to know almost overwhelming me.

'The only thing that gets you fired up—truly fired up— is your work. Your eyes light up when you're in the boardroom, challenging men and women with years of experience to better market an idea. Anneka got fired up by shopping until she dropped. The reason she was an ex-supermodel by the time she was twenty-five was because she'd gained a reputation for being unprofessional and lazy—partying and skiing were the only things she lived for. Sometimes I'd go two or three weeks without seeing her because she was too busy flying around in my jet to spend time with me.'

I frowned. 'So what on earth did you see in her? And is it even possible to shop and party that much…?' I muttered.

'Believe me, she gave it a good try. And after a few months we barely saw each other. I was about to break it off when she told me she was pregnant.'

The similarities crushed me harder. Neo and I would never have met again had it not been for the baby.

'You know how else you're different from Anneka?' he said.

I hated these comparisons. Hated the other woman's name on his lips. But I'd started this. And, for good or ill, the need to know more about what had shaped this man who made me terrified for my heart's well-being wouldn't abate.

'Enlighten me. Please.'

He ignored my droll tone, his eyes growing even more incisive as he stared at me, as if the list he was enumerating was necessary to him. Essential, even.

Maybe he needed to scrape together my *worthy* characteristics in order to be able to accept me as the mother of his child? And if he failed? If I wasn't enough? Anguish seared deeper, but he was still talking, so I forced myself to listen.

'You signed the prenup without so much as a quibble. Anneka got a team of lawyers to negotiate every clause— especially the one that stated that should I perish while we were married she would receive one hundred percent of my assets, including the funds I'd set aside for charity. Your attention to detail in the boardroom is exceptional. But I'm willing to bet you can't even remember the details of the financial package in the prenup you signed?'

I shook my head. 'The only part I cared about was what happened to our child,' I replied.

His arrogant smile widened. 'So tell me again how you plan to fleece me?'

I shrugged away the taunt, still consumed with wanting to know why he'd bothered to get together with a woman like Anneka if those were her true colours.

But I knew the answer. She was beautiful, vivacious and he'd thought she was carrying his child. It had become clear over the last few weeks that there was nothing Neo wouldn't do for his child. No sacrifice he wouldn't make.

My heart dipped in alarm and, yes, I felt a bite of jealousy at the thought that the all-encompassing feeling would never extend beyond his child. Not after what he'd experienced at the hands of another woman. Not after what I'd done to him even before our first meeting.

I was simply the vessel carrying what he wanted most in the world. How soon after I served my purpose would I be relegated to the background?

That anguishing thought drove my next question. 'So I'm a step or two up from the previous model—no pun intended. But I still have question marks over my head, don't I?'

'Don't we all?' he drawled.

'No, that's not going to fly. You've just listed the ways

I'm different from your ex, but what does that difference mean to you, Neo?' I pressed, an almost fatalistic urge smashing away my precious self-preservation.

'That remains to be seen,' he replied, and that aloofness I'd fooled myself into thinking was gone for ever resurged, saturating every inch of his perfect face.

'You mean until I prove my *worth* to you? Add the ultimate title of true mother to your child to that list? Maybe *then* you'll stop comparing me to her?'

He shrugged.

Stone-like dread settled in my midriff, depriving my lungs of air. Slowly but unrelentingly, perhaps even since that first night on Neostros, I'd allowed this thing to go beyond doing the right thing for my baby. I'd reached out, taken what I wanted for myself despite the lingering suspicion that my actions would come with emotional consequences.

And now, with this account of what had shaped him, he'd bared my own weaknesses to me.

I started to slide out of bed, froze when he reached for me.

'Where do you think you're going?'

'I'm going to shower. Alone.'

Tension rippled through his frame, his eyes narrowing to ferocious slits. 'We can't go back, Sadie. It's better you're aware of that. That you accept it.'

'You're right—we can't go back. But with your feet firmly stuck in clay you're not going to move forward either, are you?'

Again his silence spoke for him.

'Well, guess what? You may be stuck, but I'm not.'

'Explain that, if you please,' he rasped tightly.

'You're lauded for your sharp brain, Neo. Work it out for yourself.'

When I tugged myself free he released me. And that little act of setting me free, when deep down I wanted him to recapture me, drove the hard truth home.

His actions would always skew towards protecting himself. Towards shoring up his foundations with thick layers that guaranteed everyone else would remain on the outside.

Which was rather a sad and agonising state of affairs, because I very much wanted to be on the inside. So much so that when the composure that had held me together crumbled I let it, allowing the hot scald of tears to mingle with the warm shower jets. The hiss of the water muffling my quiet sobs.

But what I didn't know in those stolen, self-pitying moments was that my agony was only just starting.

*Work it out for yourself.*

I resented the unnerving panic those five words had triggered.

We were married. We'd made an agreement!

But listing her better qualities had opened my eyes to what I'd known for a while…that Sadie was truly different from Anneka. A wife a husband would be proud to possess.

But…what kind of husband? One who valued her for her brain but was too jaded to look into her heart? Perhaps because his own emotions fell short of fulfilling her needs?

Could I really stop her if she deemed me unfit to hold up my end of the bargain? If the doubts I harboured about my effectiveness as a father grew apparent?

I'd negotiated another deal in my favour by reclaiming her in my bed. One that had given me a yearning for a state I'd never considered before.

*Contentment.*

*Theos mou*, the woman I'd married was sensational. She tasted like the purest strain of innocent temptation, which would only get richer when she'd fully embraced her sensuality.

I should be pleased.

And yet, her words had only intensified that hollow sensation I'd woken up with the morning after the wedding. The feeling that had expanded ever since.

Not in a glaring, aggressive way, that could easily be identified and fixed, like a marketing flaw that required sharp intellect and an eye for detail. It had started as a ripple on the surface of a pond, effortless but determined. Unstoppable. Expanding against my will and desire to contain it.

*And you need this triple-strength protection, why?*

I ignored the wheedling voice, alarmed when I couldn't find any immediate comeback as to why I needed protection against Sadie.

Even more disturbing was the louder voice that questioned whether I was equipped to safeguard what I fought so valiantly for once my child was born. Cynicism and bitterness and being a shark in the boardroom were hardly the cornerstones of fulfilling parenthood...

Would the child I was so intent on claiming eventually resent me?

No. I would do better than the indifferent and bitter hand I'd been dealt. Just as I knew Sadie would too—if only to counteract what her own father had done to her.

The hollow sensation intensified—as if now I'd admitted one craving, several more demanded to be addressed.

Something was missing. Perhaps...within me.

Had I bargained with chips that were flawed? Pushed Sadie into marriage without stopping to examine whether I was the type of husband she wanted? A fit father for our child?

Money. Influence. Power. All things I could offer.

All things she'd rejected one by one without batting an eyelash.

Her question lingered long after she'd disappeared into the bathroom, after the hiss of the shower taunted me with the knowledge that tonight might have been the only pleasure I experienced with her.

And then, like that tree I'd known would be my doom in that moment of clarity right before the accident in Gstaad, when I heard the sharp scream from the bathroom, I suspected things would never be the same again.

When, an hour later, I stood by Sadie's bedside in another hospital, my gut twisting into knots as I stared down the barrel of a metaphorical gun, suspicion became certainty.

# CHAPTER TEN

*LOOKS MUCH WORSE than it is... Everything is fine, Mrs Xenakis. You just need to take it easy.*

I repeated the doctor's words to myself as the limo drove us home from the hospital a few hours later.

The ravaging pain shredding my heart had merely been put on hold in light of the scare in the bathroom. It was still waiting in the wings.

And even if I'd fooled myself into thinking it was in any way diminished, the tight, drawn look on Neo's face testified that our conversation in the bedroom had merely been stayed.

That determined little muscle ticking in his jaw said it all. And it had only intensified with the doctor's reassurance that our baby...*our son*...was fine. Thriving, in fact. That the blood I'd spotted in the shower was concerning, but ultimately nothing to stress over as long as I took it easy.

Why that news had triggered Neo's ashen complexion and lockjawed determination only served to expand the stone lodged in my heart.

Had our conversation and the scare merely fast-tracked the inevitable?

We completed the journey home in tight, fraught silence.

When the driver shut off the ignition, Neo strode around to my side, offered his hand in silent command. I took it, stepped out, but when he leaned forward to lift me up I threw out a halting hand.

So soon after everything I'd experienced in his bed, and afterwards, having him so close would be detrimental to my emotional well-being.

*The very thing I should've guarded against in the first place.*

'I can walk on my own. The doctor said to take it easy. I think that safely includes walking from the car to the villa,' I said, unable to keep the tightness from my voice.

His lips tightened and he stayed close, unbearably surrounding me with his heat as I climbed the stairs to my suite, then perched on the wide, striped divan and watched the staff fuss with a tray of food and soft drinks Neo must have ordered before we left the hospital.

When the housekeeper lingered, Neo dragged an impatient hand through his hair. 'Leave us,' he snapped, authority stamped in his voice that saw his command immediately obeyed. He paced to the door, shut it, then returned, his footsteps heavy and resolute.

I knew what was coming. Unlike that postcard that had torn my world apart, this heartache-shaped wrecking ball I could see coming from a mile away.

'Don't do it. Whatever you're about to say, don't say it, Neo,' I blurted.

He froze beside the bed, then dragged his hands down his face. Even with two-day stubble and shadows haunting his turbulent eyes, he looked sublime.

The man I craved more than was wise for me.

The man I'd fallen in love with as he glared at me from across his office, tossing bullet-sharp questions about marketing and then reproducing a birthday cupcake at short notice in the most stunning setting on earth.

'Do you know what it felt like to see you there on that bathroom floor?' he demanded raggedly, his voice rough to the point of near incoherence.

My pain twisted, morphed, as a new strand was woven into its jagged fabric. 'Every pregnancy carries a risk. The doctor just said that.'

He gave a violent shake of his head. 'It wouldn't have happened if I'd kept my hands to myself! If I hadn't pushed for more!'

'You don't know that.'

'I do. I feel it, Sadie. Right here.' He pounded his closed fist on his midriff, his jaw tight with recrimination.

'You think you're something special?'

He inhaled sharply. 'What?'

'You think we're the only couple who indulge in sex during pregnancy? That you deserve some kind of special punishment for doing something that comes naturally?'

His gaze turned bleak. 'I can't speak for others, but I know what my actions came close to costing me. The way I've been with you, right from the start, herding you into decisions you were reluctant to take—'

'There you go again—seeking the crown of martyrdom. I have a voice, Neo. And, if you recall, you didn't get everything your own way. What makes you think I didn't want it too? That I wasn't in a hurry to fall into bed with you or marry you for my own reasons?'

He shook his head. 'Be that as it may, I set this ball rolling—'

'What? Gave me a roof over my head? A job opportunity that most would give their eye teeth for?'

'You said yourself—those are just things. What you could've lost—'

'But *we* didn't *lose* anything, Neo. Our baby is fine.'

Raw bitterness tightened his face. 'But for how long?'

My heart shredded. 'What?'

'I only negotiated for the short term, Sadie. As unfortunate as the circumstances are, it's a wake-up call. I need to accept that I don't have the tools for the long term.'

My fists bunched as anguish ripped through me. 'I don't buy that either, Neo. But I can't stop you from this path you obviously want to take, so just spare me the suspense and spit it out?'

His jaw worked for the longest time. Then he nodded. 'I'm leaving for Brazil tomorrow. Then travelling in Latin America for the next few weeks.'

'You're leaving.'

It wasn't a question. More absorbing the impact of the wrecking ball.

'Yes.'

'Because I'm *so different* from Anneka?' I taunted sarcastically.

'Yes!' The word was drawn from his soul. Almost as if he was terrified to admit it.

My jaw dropped. 'Neo…'

'You'll be taken care of—'

'I don't want a laundry list of things you're putting in place to ensure I don't lift a finger. I want to know why you promised me better terms and are now reneging.'

'This is for your own good.'

I couldn't help the laughter that spilled out. 'Is it, though? You know what you remind me of, Neo? My father. Always looking for something better! You changed the rules to suit you when you decided you wanted a wife, not just in name, but in your bed. Then you changed them again because you can't handle a little challenge. I've outlived my usefulness to you in one area. So you're shelving me until you get the other things that you want.'

His jaw clenched. 'No—what your father did, he did for himself. What I'm doing is for *you*.'

'Trust me to know my own mind! Believe me when I tell you what's in my heart.'

He lost another layer of colour, but his eyes blazed with quiet fury. 'I've made my decision. But know that besides my absence, nothing changes.'

'That's where you're wrong. *I've* changed. I know my own worth now. I know I want more than this. I won't be bargained with, or put on a shelf to suit you. So if you think your world is going to stay trouble-free because you've laid down the law, think again.'

'What's that supposed to mean?'

I shrugged dismissively, even though it was the last thing I felt like doing. 'I guess we'll find out. Goodbye, Neo.'

He stayed put, his gaze fixed in that way that said he was assessing me for weakness.

And because I wasn't sure how long I could stay put without cracking, I turned away from him, closed my eyes and simply pretended he wasn't there.

I heard the ominous snick of the door a minute later.

Then the tears fell—long and hard and shattering.

It was supposed to work.

The punishing schedule.

The soul-sucking jet lag.

The endless meetings.

Hell, even barking at executives was supposed to make me feel better. To fuel the conviction that I was doing the right thing.

She'd accused me of being like her father. Initially it had provided sustaining anger, and I'd burned in the righteousness of believing myself the exact opposite.

But, as relentless as time's march, the kernel of truth had expanded…like a weird, never-ending concentric circle that echoed its presence in my quiet moments.

First I'd used her to salve the bad news she'd delivered. Then, from the moment she'd announced she was carrying my child, I'd pinned her to me—my last hope of fatherhood and I was determined to have it, regardless of the fact that I lacked the effective tools to be a father. And during the process, I'd hammered out an agreement that bound her to me only until I had what I wanted.

And when I'd decided I wanted more, I'd worked on the problem until she'd fallen into my arms.

Only then had I realised the full impact of *more*. That, while I could give her every material and carnal pleasure she desired, *I* was the one who was too greedy. Too selfish. Because I'd never stopped to think that she would want more too. Or that I was equipped to deal with her demand.

Fate had given me the rudest wake-up call. And, as much

as every moment of breathing turned me inside out, Sadie deserved for me to stay away. She deserved the peace to bear her child without my greedy, demanding presence. Without the wants and needs and longings that clawed at me every hour of every day, sullying her beautiful existence.

So what if the thought of going another minute, another hour, without seeing her face killed me?

*You'll simply have to suffer!*

My intercom sounded, ripping another curse from my throat.

'I was quite explicit in my desire not to be disturbed.'

Because I deserved at least ten minutes of undiluted torment each hour, even as other minutes provided unending agony.

'Yes, sir, but I thought you should know—'

'Save your breath. Warning him won't do any good.'

I jackknifed up from my position against the dark wall in my office. Took a step forward and steadied myself against the dizzying effect of her.

Two long weeks during which only the security cameras installed at the villa had provided woefully brief glimpses of this goddess who carried my child. During which daily reports of her improved health and blooming pregnancy had sustained my raging hunger for her.

*And now she was here.*

A vision in white cotton that clung to her bust, her hips and, *Christos*, the magnificent protrusion of her belly. Her hair was twisted into an elaborate crown on top of her head, further proclaiming her celestial status.

It was all I could do not to fall at her feet in sublime worship of her, this woman who held a heart unworthy of her. This woman who'd exploded into my life and claimed a place in it I never wanted back.

God, would I ever get over the impact of Neo Xenakis?

I doubted it.

Or else every single vow I'd taken and every form of punishment I'd devised for myself in a wild bid to stop thinking about him, stop dreaming about him, would have worked.

Instead, each day had brought a bracing kind of hell. A craving that went against all common sense.

I'd driven Callie quite mad with my pathetic stoicism. While I wanted to blame her for appointing herself chief nursemaid, I'd eventually taken pity on her—succumbed when she'd called up the Xenakis jet and arranged an intercontinental flight, along with a doctor, much to the chagrin of her husband.

From Neo's poleaxed expression now, Axios had kept the secret.

The look was morphing, though, the shock wearing off.

His gaze rushed over me and he paled a little before his eyes narrowed. 'What are you doing here?' he bit out.

Despite its tension, the sound of his voice sent tingles down my spine.

I closed the gap between us by another few steps, my heart kicking against my ribs when his eyes dropped to my distended stomach.

'I work for this company, remember? Unless those privileges have been revoked too?'

'You know exactly what I mean. You should be resting. In Athens. Not…not…' He stopped. Frowned.

'Have you forgotten where you are?' I asked. 'You're in Costa Rica…negotiating to buy the country's second-largest airline.'

His frown intensified. 'Thanks for the reminder. My statement still stands.'

'Does it? Perhaps if you'd been at home I wouldn't have needed to cross continents to have a conversation with you.'

His mouth worked and he swallowed noisily. 'Sadie—'

'No.' I took another few steps, then stopped when his aftershave hit me like a brick of sensation. 'You don't get to speak. Not until I've said what's on my mind. And even then, the jury's out as to whether I want to hear what you have to say.'

'This is the third time you've stormed my office since we met.'

'It seems to be the only place where I can get through to you.'

A raw gleam lit his grey eyes before his expression tightened. 'That's not entirely true. But, *parakalo*, whatever you have to say to me, do it while sitting down?'

'And ruin this superb effect I'm having on you?'

His fist tightened with the blatant need to bodily compel me to the sofa. 'What do you want, Sadie?'

'For you to come home. Or give me a divorce.'

He lost another shade of colour. 'What?'

'Two choices. Take one or the other. But I'm not leaving here without an answer.'

'You dare to—'

'Oh, I do. Very much. Because you know what? I've decided there's nothing you can do to me. Sue the mother of your child? I think not. Toss me out of your company? I'll just find another job, because I'm good at what I do. But I don't think you want to lose my professional skills either. Really, all that's standing in our way is *you*.'

His breathing intensified and he looked, shockingly, as if he was on the brink of hyperventilating. 'You think any of this has been easy, Sadie?'

The raw note in his voice caught at that vulnerable spot I'd never been able to protect, ever since our first meeting.

I stepped into his space, uncaring for my own heart, and glared with everything I had. 'You walked away. And stayed away. You tell me.'

'It's been torture!' he yelled. 'I reach for you at night and you're not there. I turn to throw a question at you in the boardroom and find some lame executive staring back at me. You've ruined me for everything! For everyone! You were supposed to bewitch me for a little while. Until I satisfied the craving you triggered. Instead you're all I think about—every second of every day.'

My heart swan-dived right to my toes, then dared to beat its wings faster, to climb and climb and *hope*.

'Keep…keep talking.'

'That night, when you accused me of not moving forward, I couldn't answer your charge because somewhere along the line I'd gone from holding you to a higher standard to recognising that I couldn't meet those standards myself.'

'What are you *talking* about?'

'I've held myself back from giving my all emotionally all my life, Sadie. My grandfather did and look where he ended up. When Anneka told me she was pregnant I immediately offered her my name and my wealth, but nothing else. I knew I didn't love her and, aside from her betrayal and the lesson that delivered, I haven't spared her a thought since I threw her out of my life. But you…'

He stopped, swallowed.

'I spent weeks after our first meeting unable to get you out of my mind. When you turned up in my office in Athens I thought you felt the same. That you'd simply been better at plotting a reconnection.'

'Instead I dropped another bombshell in your life.'

He shook his head, jerked closer until we were breathing the same air. 'Instead you held out your hands and presented me with the most precious gift any man who wishes to be a father could ask for.'

'So you believe our baby is yours?'

'I believed you before we landed back in London that day. A woman who goes to great pains to admit her wrongdoing when she could have run a mile and passed the blame to others is a woman of integrity, in my book. Even when I gave you the chance to pass the blame on to your boss, you didn't.'

'If you knew all that, then why?'

He shrugged, that domineering alpha male rising to the

fore. 'Because I'm a negotiator, Sadie. I played my cards close to my chest to gain the upper hand. I wanted our child, but I wanted you even more. I could've dispatched you back to London, had a security team watch you and swoop in to negotiate terms of custody once the baby was born.'

'But you didn't because you *wanted* me? Past tense?'

'Oh, no, *glikia mou*. Not even close to past tense. It's very present. Very real. So much it scares me.'

Something electric lit up inside me. 'Is that why you're hiding here on the other side of the world? Because you're scared?'

'I'm here because I don't deserve you. As much as I want to negotiate my way back to you, I can't stand the possibility that you'll wake up one day and be disappointed.'

'My God. You've put us through all this suffering because for the first time in your life you're experiencing the very human emotion of self-doubt?'

He frowned. 'Sadie, this isn't a flimsy—'

'You think I wasn't scared to death when I realised I was in love with you? That I haven't wanted to tear my hair out to see if it would bring me a moment's relief from the constant ache of loving you and not knowing whether you love me back?'

His gorgeous lips dropped open in shock. '*Christos*, Sadie. I—'

'I'm a pregnant woman nearing her third trimester, Neo. The next words out of your mouth had better be words I want to hear.'

His arms darted out, caught me to him, as if he was afraid I'd flee when in fact my legs were threatening to stop supporting me.

'Let's get one thing clear. You're never to touch a hair on your head with an aim of tearing it out. Ever. But, more importantly, Sadie…if this madness inside me that yearns only for you, if this heart that beats true only when you're near, means this is love, then I love you. And if it's not, if

I get it wrong somewhere along the way, I know I'll have you there to steer me true. For a chance to be at your side through this life I will leave the negotiations to you, follow your lead. Show me how to love, Sadie, and I will be your apt pupil for the rest of our lives.'

The depth of his promise took the last ounce of strength from my legs. He caught me up, as I knew he would, strode over to the sofa and sank into it.

'Okay, if that's what it takes. Here's your first lesson. You never leave me behind again.'

'I vow it,' he replied, with feeling.

I rearranged myself in his lap, framed his face between my hands. 'You bring any doubts you have to me. We fix and grow and love together. But most of all, Neo, you just open your heart, let me love you and our baby. We'll be the best versions of ourselves we can be for our family and trust the rest to take care of itself. Will you do that?'

A suspicious sheen glistened in his eyes. But he didn't look away, didn't blink it back. He just stared into my eyes and nodded. 'You have yourself a deal, *amorfo mou.*'

'Good. Now, please kiss me. Then please take me home.'

# EPILOGUE

'IT'S TIME, NEO.'

Heels clicked closer as my wife entered our bedroom and crossed over to where I stood at the window.

'Our guests are wondering if the two of you are planning to join the festivities—especially since you're holding the guest of honour hostage,' she teased.

I was torn between staring at the vision Sadie created in her white Grecian-style dress and the precious bundle I held in my arms.

With her flaming hair piled on top of her head in an elaborate knot, and the skin I'd explored thoroughly just a few hours ago glowing, Sadie won the attention-grabbing stakes. But only by a fraction.

My son—*thee mou*, would I ever stop being awed by the miracle of him?—three months old and in good health, came a very close second.

'Five more minutes?' I cradled his warmth closer, unwilling to share him just yet.

Sadie shook her head, smiling widely as she approached, her swaying hips wreaking havoc with my breathing.

'You said that twenty minutes ago. I know you don't care what anyone else thinks, but I have a good brownie point system going with your family. I don't want to ruin it.'

'Impossible. Every person out there loves you—they wouldn't been invited to Helios's christening otherwise.'

Her beautiful eyes widened. 'You didn't have Wendell vet them, did you?'

I shrugged. 'Maybe…'

She laughed, and the sound burrowed deep, stirring emotions I hadn't imagined I could experience just a handful of months ago.

But then, so many things had changed since that day in Costa Rica. Sadie had introduced me to the phenomenon of unconditional love, her giving heart and fearless love challenging mine to reciprocate. And the result continued to astound me daily. Even the atmosphere of cool indifference with my parents had began to thaw under Sadie's expert guidance.

She insisted the birth of our miracle son was the reason.

I disagreed.

'Well, just to let you know, our mothers are *this* close to staging a break-in to claim their grandson,' she said with a stunning smile. 'I estimate you have about a minute.'

'Then I'll make the most of it. Come to me, *agape mou*,' I murmured, greedy for more of this soul-stirring feeling.

'I love it when you call me that,' she said when she reached me, one hand sliding around my waist, her other caressing Helios's black-maned head. 'He's so beautiful—our little miracle.'

The overwhelming love and wonder I felt was echoed in her voice.

'He's as beautiful as his exceptional mama, but *moro mou*, you're our miracle, Sadie. Without you, our lives wouldn't be this full, mine changed for ever for the better,' I said.

Beautiful green eyes blinked back tears, and when she went on tiptoe to kiss me I met her halfway, revelling in the supreme contentment that this gorgeous creature was mine. That she had given me a son despite my doctors still scratching their heads over tests that showed such a feat was impossible.

Their verdict was that Helios might be the only child Sadie and I would have. But who were they to make pronouncements? I already had the miracle of love and fatherhood. Nothing was impossible.

When we broke the kiss Sadie sighed, resting her head

on my shoulder. 'Okay, Neo. Five more minutes. But I get to stay too.'

As if I would let her go.

'*Agapita*, you should know by now that I wouldn't have it any other way.'

\* \* \* \* \*

# LET'S TALK
# *Romance*

For exclusive extracts, competitions
and special offers, find us online:

- **f** facebook.com/millsandboon
- **⊡** @millsandboonuk
- **🐦** @millsandboon

Or get in touch on 0844 844 1351*

For all the latest titles coming soon,
visit millsandboon.co.uk/nextmonth